GOOD AND EVIL AND OTHER STORIES

Samanta Schweblin

Translated by Megan McDowell

PICADOR

First published 2025 by Alfred A. Knopf,
a division of Penguin Random House LLC, New York

First published in the UK 2025 by Picador

This paperback edition first published 2026 by Picador
an imprint of Pan Macmillan
The Smithson, 6 Briset Street, London EC1M 5NR
EU representative: Macmillan Publishers Ireland Ltd, 1st Floor,
The Liffey Trust Centre, 117–126 Sheriff Street Upper,
Dublin 1 D01 YC43
Associated companies throughout the world

ISBN 978-1-0350-5018-5

Originally published in Spanish as *El Buen Mal* by Planeta S.A.
and Literatura Random House in 2025.
'An Eye in the Throat' was first published in *The Paris Review*, Issue 247,
translated by Megan McDowell.
'A Visit from the Chief' was first published in *The New Yorker*,
February 2025, translated by Megan McDowell.

1 3 5 7 9 8 6 4 2

A CIP catalogue record for this book is available from the British Library.

Printed and bound in the UK using 100% Renewable Electricity
by CPI Group (UK) Ltd

MIX
Paper | Supporting
responsible forestry
FSC® C116313
FSC
www.fsc.org

Strange is always truer.

—Silvina Ocampo, *Letters*

CONTENTS

WELCOME TO THE CLUB

I jump into the water from the end of the pier and sink down, holding my nose. After the initial impact I open my eyes, surrendering to the fall as it grows softer, and to the colors all around me that seem new, denser, and more iridescent. I descend, holding my breath.

Maybe a minute passes. Finally, slowly, my feet touch the mossy ground, like I'm an astronaut landing on the moon. I let go of my nose and lower my arms, and my body tenses up. A contraction comes from my lungs, a spasm, and I wait a little longer. I touch the rocks tied to my waist; the knot can always be untied. Perhaps to keep from changing my mind, I inhale. I fill my chest with water and a new, hard cold hits my ribs. I want this to happen painlessly. A dozen bubbles escape from my mouth and nose and rise upward. Another spasm suddenly wracks me and I'm afraid of what might happen now. I let out my remaining air. I'm struck by the liquid feeling where there was always oxygen before, but above all I'm struck by how lucid I feel. How calm. I look at my hands, larger and whiter than they were above-water, and wonder how long it will take to lose consciousness. Algae, schools of silvery eyes, plankton floating like glitter. My body feels loose, and an extraordinary sensation arises from the contact with warm currents, cool ones, warm again. In the distance, the lake floor grows murky. How much time has passed? Three minutes, five—it's something I no longer know how to calculate. I was sure this would happen faster.

I touch the rocks, feeling for the knot. I'm not changing my mind; at this point, what's done is done. It's curiosity. I untie the rope and the rocks fall away. Their impact causes an earthquake near my feet, which slowly lift off the ground. I stay there, sort of floating, unsure what to do. And it's then, at that moment, when I remember thinking, *What if this is it?* To float and wonder for the rest of eternity: the first real fear I have that day. To be unable to move forward or backward, ever again, in any direction.

I curl up, kick against the ground to push upward. What was it that went wrong? I'm trying to understand. For a moment ascending seems easy, but after a few feet my body stops, comfortable in its levitation. It takes a while to return, to finally reach the more crystalline warmth of the surface. Will I breathe again when I emerge from the water? I wonder if anyone is looking for me, and I fear a scene. My arms take a few strokes, my head finally leaves the water, and I feel the relief of cold air on my wet face.

The rocky shore is as empty as ever, and I paddle over to the log ladder and climb up onto the pier. I retch, leaning over the deck, expecting to throw up all the water, but nothing happens. The hot wood immediately absorbs the drops falling from my chin. I try to stand but my body is weak and lax, so I wait a moment and try again. Across the garden, the sun bounces off the house's windows and stings my eyes. I wring out my hair, try to do the same with the front of my shirt, the cuffs of my pants, and walk to the other end of the pier. My sandals are still in the grass, right where I left them. I slip them on and struggle up the embankment to cross the garden uphill.

I remember how I reach the house. I look at my reflection in the glass of the back door, my wet clothes stuck to my body, my hand approaching to slide open the glass that squeaks on the runner, the frame that crosses in front of my eyes and carries off my reflection, and past it the living room, the dining room table with the remains of breakfast still uncleared. I lean against the doorway and, with a final effort, cross the threshold.

Inside, everything is calm. The hydrangeas I cut in the morning are undisturbed in the two kitchen vases. I pick up the letters I'd left propped against the vases, one I wrote for him and one for the girls. I'm not sure whether picking up those letters is a good decision. I'm not even sure if taking them from this table means taking them from the same table where I left them a while ago. I'm not sure of anything, not then and not now, but the clock is already showing twelve twenty, so I go up to the bedroom, put the letters in the nightstand drawer, take off my wet clothes and put on dry ones, and go back down to make lunch.

They pull up honking the horn and the girls roll into the house like a whirlwind. They're carrying a big cage that holds a rabbit.

"We have to take care of it until Thursday," my husband says. "One week per family."

I'm beating eggs. It takes an enormous effort, but I'm trembling and I trust the action will hide my state. The girls wrap their arms around my waist, and I have to lift the bowl higher so I can see their faces.

"His name is Blimp."

"Yeah! Blimp."

Their voices echo in my head. The older one presses her nose into my stomach and inhales deeply.

"Mommy, you smell bad."

The younger one copies her.

"You do! Like dirty mud."

"All right," I tell them, "let's eat."

I remember how afraid I am to stop beating the eggs. But I stop and nothing happens, no one looks at me. My older daughter pushes the cage against the wall and frees the rabbit. Her father hurries to close the sliding glass door. When he comes back he summons us with three claps of his hands.

"From now on, we keep all the doors closed," he says.

I start the fifth omelet in the skillet and serve the ones that are ready. My husband knows he's in charge of the one that is still on the burner because he's the only one who eats two. So we sit down at the table, and the girls' silence as they take the first bites helps me finally feel calm, at least for a few seconds.

Everything is in order, I tell myself. *Easy now.*

I sit watching the rabbit as, without any real caution or circumspection, it hops across the dining room to its dish of water on the floor. If Blimp is an expert traveler in new lands, I am this woman anchored always in the same place. Blimp comes over and sniffs at my feet. His nose tickles, and just to be on the safe side I grab on to the edge of the table.

"His name's Blimp 'cause he's fat."

"Nuh-uh, that's not why."

"Yeah it is, the teacher said so."

The girls sword fight with their forks for a moment and then go on eating. My husband gets up for the last omelet, and on the way there he's already making a phone call.

Everything is in order, I tell myself, and the pleasure from the tickling nose surprises me.

"Mommy, are you happy?"

With her silverware held aloft, my youngest waits eagerly for my answer. Suddenly she jumps down from her chair and runs around the table without ever lowering her knife and fork.

"Blimpy! Blimpy! Mommy's happy!"

"But eating would be too much to ask, huh?" my husband says when he comes back with his second omelet, noticing the untouched food on my plate.

My oldest watches and listens. The worst part is whatever it is that she's learning from us.

Lunch ends and my family disappears up the stairs. I like this house because of its porous ability to absorb us all into its rooms. In the living room, the cage has been left open and empty, and I'm comforted by the thought of the girls playing with Blimp, entertained in my absence. It's like when I can hear the washing machine or the microwave in the background—I relax because, even if I can't take action myself, something practical is still getting done.

I go back to the sliding glass door and gaze out at the garden. Everything that's happening seems possible, but how can it be possible? How can it be that what happened, happened, and I still feel so fine, and even my hair is drying? I breathe, take my purse from the coatrack, and go out the front door. Once again, his car is parked diagonally in the driveway; it's like a barricade. We don't argue about that anymore. I've learned to slide my legs between the fender and the wall almost without getting my clothes dirty. When he is home, "going out" is like "overcoming," like "vanquishing" the doorway; if I want to get through it I have to really be determined.

The next-door neighbor is pulling up in his truck. This is the day I understand what it is he really does. But for now I just think he's coming back from hunting, like all the days when he wears his cap with the visor forward. He has a pair of buck horns hanging over the porch door, and though he's not a military man, he dresses like one.

Three years ago he was on the front page of the local paper for a harassment case brought by a woman who used to work in Toni's café. After that article, we never saw her again. And then the thing with the barbed wire happened. We tried to talk to him the day he put it up, explaining several times that the girls could get hurt if they played too close to it. He said that was why the wire was barbed, that it was the only way parents would be sure to keep their children away.

"The wire is for the parents," he said.

I remember how, during the course of this day, there are many things I try not to think about. At first, the neighbor is on that list.

Outside, in the shade of the trees, the heat is less stifling. On the corner I ring Daniela's doorbell and try to fix my appearance a little. I comb my fingers through my hair and find a piece of still-wet algae tangled in the ends. It stretches out like gum when I tug at it. I drop it on the ground and wipe my hands on my pants, then ring the bell again. No one answers. When I get tired of waiting, I go down to the square.

The neighborhood still seems just as exaggeratedly big and moneyed as the first day we arrived, several years ago now. A couple of blocks down is the café. Inside, two tables are occupied and Toni is washing dishes in the kitchen. I see him through the little window and he winks at me. I poke my head in and ask about Daniela, but he doesn't know where she is, so I sit down for a minute at the counter. A while back, Toni and I had sex a few times, on the kitchen floor, in the changing room, and in the employee bathroom. And then one day Toni said, "Okay, that'll do it, right?" He said it wearily, as if he'd been scrubbing at a stain for a long time and still couldn't get it out, and now he was finally giving up.

A woman comes over, picks up a sugar dispenser, and smiles at me before returning to her table. I touch my hair to be sure there is no more algae in it. I find a little strip, maybe a leftover bit of the other piece, but I don't think anyone has noticed. I'm relieved to see that no one detects anything strange, and it makes me want to stand up and stretch my limbs, do something other than sit here waiting.

I go outside and smoke a cigarette. A car pulls in from the main entrance, passes the café, and drives off. The sidewalk has no columns or walls or posts to lean against—that's what we all have houses for. The street is just one long yard we can walk through. In the square, I sit down on the bench. I remember thinking that I'll count to ten, and if I still feel like it, I'll light another cigarette. I count so as not to think.

Just then I see the rabbit cross the street: a bunny that is fat enough to be named Blimp. He flees into the bushes. Then I see one of the girls. She is crying and clutching at her head, her face red and her nose running, the anguish so consuming her that the task of searching for the rabbit becomes impossible. Will she inherit my stunted emotional intelligence? The younger one comes behind her, copying her sister's expressions but not crying, her attentive eyes peering into every corner. I stand up and walk toward them. Their father is trailing after them, phone dangling from his hand.

"You left the sliding door open," he says.

"Mom! Blimp!"

The younger one hugs me. The older one cries.

"What are we gonna do, Mommy?"

We split up, him with the younger girl, me with the older, one team on either side of the street, shaking bushes between the neighbors' yards. Once, from the kitchen, I saw a couple of bums doing something similar in my own front yard. I don't know what they were looking for. I called security, and someone came and took them away. But a woman's yellow sweater was left hanging on the rosebush for almost a week. In the end I picked it up and put it in the washing machine, by itself and on the fastest setting. I dried it, folded it, carried it the seven blocks to the bus stop, and left it there on the bench. I understood that wasn't exactly the same as returning it, but at least I was putting it somewhere. I didn't want things that didn't belong to me in the house.

We move on to the next house's yard. A neighbor peers out the window. I recognize her as the mother of the twins in my younger daughter's class. She'll come out and help us, I think. She'll ask, "What happened?" And she'll say, "I saw the bunny!" She peers at me and turns away from the window, and I look toward the door expecting her to come out any second. Once, in front of the school entrance, each of her hands holding one of my daughters', she told me, "This is the last time I'm waiting for you, understand? You're not the only one making a big effort around here."

But the door to her house doesn't open.

My daughter catches up with me through the bushes and hugs me, and with her hug she also pushes me. We cross another yard. When her father gets tired of searching, he claps three times. The family gathers in the middle of the street and we go back to the house. He is annoyed, I can tell by the tone of his voice.

"I know where we can get another rabbit," he says.

He says it right in front of the girls, and suddenly four little hands clutch me tightly.

"No. No, no! Blimpy!"

We are at our driveway when, behind my husband's back, I see our neighbor walking toward us.

"Hello," he says.

Only then does my husband turn and see the neighbor. He is carrying the rabbit by its ears.

"Is he dead, Mom? Mommy!"

The girls hop anxiously around us. The rabbit kicks in the air and then surrenders again to the swaying.

"What if that hurts him?" my youngest asks.

"That's how you carry rabbits," my husband reassures them.

But Blimp is too fat, and the man is close enough now that we can see the force in the tendons of that fist, the animal's mouth stretched into a cruel smile, teeth sticking out, eyes narrowed and weepy.

"Who wants rabbit for dinner?" asks the man.

The girls scream. The man laughs.

"Here, take it, I come in peace."

He holds out the rabbit toward us. My husband tries to receive it, but doesn't know how.

"You have to put the phone down to take the rabbit," the man says.

I hear his words and smile, despite the distaste I feel for him. And when the rabbit finally changes hands, and the girls let go of me and run to their father, and he kneels down to reunite them with Blimp, the man turns toward me, gazes at me for a moment, and then frowns.

"What's wrong?" He looks at my mouth, my eyes, my hair.

"It's the girls' rabbit," I say. "Well, the school's rabbit, and—"

"I mean with you. Are you okay?"

He takes a step toward me. I think of the algae and run a hand through my hair. I glance at my family to be sure that they're walking away now.

"Nothing's wrong," I say. "It's just that I saw you with the rabbit and it startled me, I know how you like to hunt . . ."

"You think I hunt because I like it?"

He smiles, but he's every bit as annoyed as my husband. He shakes his head slowly and never takes his eyes off of me.

"It's really something to see you so self-righteous, after what you did this morning."

It's as if he had grabbed me by the throat with both hands. As if now he were waiting, without ever loosening his grip. *He saw me,* I think to myself. I remember how I think that he saw me, and how I can't think about anything else, not about the rabbit or the girls or about what's going to happen later. He takes another step toward me and he's too close now. His finger is pointing to the middle of my chest.

"You think you can do whatever you please and then just change your mind?"

I glance around for my family, but they're gone.

"Do you really think that's how it works?"

I take a step backward.

"Where are you going?"

I try to answer, but I can only step back again.

"Hey! Wait, listen to me."

I retreat another step, and another. I walk away from the man, and every time I turn to look at him, he is still standing there, watching me. I walk fast, now without glancing back. I overcome the barricade, enter the house, close the door. Since this is my house, there are things to lean on, columns and walls. I spend some time regaining my composure.

The sliding glass door is closed now and the girls are playing, chasing after Blimp. Soon the house reabsorbs its inhabitants into the rooms, releasing us in shifts and catching us again. After dinner, my husband goes into his study to work and I send the girls to bed. It takes a while for them to calm down, and the youngest is the last to fall asleep. When she finally closes her eyes, I wait for a while sitting beside her, looking at her. Then I focus on my feet, because there is still dried, greenish mud between my toes. I take off my flip-flops and sniff them. I want to shower, get rid of this smell, put on my pajamas, and lie down, but I realize I'm not capable of doing any of that. Every time I think of the neighbor, my throat closes up again. Finally, I gather my strength and stand up. I remember how I go down the stairs: telling myself, *You have to move this leg, you have to move the other,* reminding myself how to breathe, and, for the first time that day, a day I will never forget, giving myself an instruction.

I leave the house again, maneuver past the car barricade to reach the street. The man is sitting on his porch steps. It's the only fenced-in lot on the block, but when I get closer I see that, this time, the gate is ajar. I push it open and enter. He waits without moving as I approach. Two bright motion-activated lights come on and illuminate the yard. At his feet there are three buckets, dirty rags, and some tools. A few seconds later the lights go off again.

"I was waiting for you," he says. He is holding a half-empty beer.

He offers me a beer, too, opens it, and hands it to me.

"I'm sorry if I was rude. I lose my patience quickly," he says.

I take the bottle. "Don't worry about it."

He watches me until I take a sip. I know he wants me to say something more. In my house the light in our bedroom goes out and everything grows a little darker. The man finishes his beer.

"I'm listening."

Does he want an explanation? Does he want me to ask a question? I think of the pier and the almost painful need to vomit up water, even though my mouth is completely dry.

"If you don't have anything to say," he juts his chin toward my house, "you can go. I've got enough on my hands."

He waits in silence while I try to understand what I came here for. I remember that before putting the girls to bed, I opened the sliding door again, and I held on to its frame so hard that I could feel my tendons stiffen. I felt my entire body wanting to let go and take off running again to the lake, and I was certain that, if I did let go, I wouldn't be able to stop it.

"It's as if . . ." I spread out my fingers and look at my hands.

He nods, pats a step in an invitation to sit down. I settle in beside him.

"As if I were still sinking."

He drags one of the buckets toward him, takes a knife from among the tools, puts his hands into the bucket, and starts to work. He has something in his hands, diffuse in the shadow.

"I'm afraid that . . ." I search deliberately for the words, because I want him to understand.

"You have to get used to it," he orders, and spits to one side.

He works in the bucket; there is blood between his fingers, on his wrists. He takes the knife out of the bucket and scratches his chin with the back of his hand. He is skinning a small animal, pulling off the hide, and the blade moves gently over red leg muscles.

"Give it a try," he says.

Without a pause in his work, he pushes another bucket toward me with his foot.

"Your knife is already inside."

I almost expect to find my kitchen knife there. Finding something like that would scare me even more than what I am presumedly about to do.

"The first cut has to go from end to end."

He leans toward me and with his other hand pulls a hare from my bucket, holds it by the legs head down, steady at my eye level. It's an extraordinarily long animal, and its head has already been cut off.

"You have to open it like a book. If you have trouble doing it from the neck, open it at the belly, and from there go up and then down. Then you just have to pull, the skin comes right off."

He moves his hands over the animal to show me the correct directions, and that's how I get a good look at his wrist: two long scars, thick like worms. He drops the hare inside my bucket and goes back to work.

The knife he calls "mine" is small and has a marble handle. I hold it, and that's all I can do.

"How did you do it?" I ask without looking at him, because maybe I don't know what I'm asking, or I'm ashamed, or I'd rather not know. He doesn't reply, so I wait. "Get used to it, I mean, and keep going."

"I'm telling you."

I listen as closely as I can. We are two simians in clothes, hands hanging down inside our buckets. He indicates mine with a tilt of his head.

"I'm lending you this one for practice. But you have your own rabbit."

He puts down the knife.

"I don't understand," I say. I need him to be clearer, to say things word by word.

He opens another beer and takes a sip.

"You think I had anyone to explain to me how this works?"

I don't answer. He moves his beer close to my chest and hits my sternum with the base of the bottle. It's a soft tap, but it almost makes my heart stop.

"You want to jump in the water with a sinker of rocks tied to your waist?"

He's saying it, now he is. All those words.

"All right, if that's what you want, fine. You want to parade around among the living like nothing happened? Also fine: welcome to the club."

What I want is for him to skin me, I want to put my hands into the bucket and let the pain snuff me out completely.

"But you have to pay a price."

He yanks a long strip of skin upward, until it comes all the way off, and he returns it to the bucket.

"Why? I didn't do anything to anyone."

"Really? Is that really what you think?"

I stand up, setting my half-finished beer on the ground.

"You have to pay," he says.

I shake my head, and without realizing it I'm walking away. I am furious.

"Hey!" he says.

The lights in the yard come on. For a few seconds everything is so bright that I have to cover my eyes with an arm. My hardened tendons, as if they were still gripping the sliding-door frame, remind me that I could still let go and start running again toward the lake. Under my arm, the man is working in his bucket. I go back toward him.

"Please," I say. But it's as if I'd said, *Grab me by the neck and strangle me right now;* it's as if I'd said, *I beg you, I know you're capable.* "Please," I say, "please speak clearly and tell me what you have to say."

The man takes the handles of all three buckets so they hang from his right hand, then stands up.

"I have to put up with all your prejudices." He walks toward the garage and I follow.

"What prejudices? What are you talking about?"

"You think I hunt for pleasure, you think I just love my barbed wire fence. You think everyone around here is a little cruel to you, and you, on the other hand, are chock-full of good intentions."

He goes into the garage and sets the three buckets on a big wooden workbench. There are animal skins hung from two long beams, drying.

"Please," I say. "Something's wrong, I know something is really wrong."

Inside the garage there is almost no light.

"I can't hold on," I say to the man. "I can't take any more."

"You have to hold on."

"I don't know how to. I'm begging you."

He takes my hand by the wrist and forces it palm-down on the table. *Now he's going to cut off my fingers,* I think, *he's going to skin me.*

"The first thing is to calm down." He takes my other hand and places it on the table too.

The wood is wet and dirty, scarred from so much use, but it's strong, and I understand that it is helping me stay on my feet. What if I'm going crazy? It's the first time I've asked myself that question, and it almost feels like making a wish: if I'm crazy, all I have to do is manage to get back home.

"From now on you have to learn to hold yourself up."

It's logical. It makes so much sense. He takes me by the arm.

"It's something you have to do every day. Understand?"

I have to get back home.

"Every day. If there's one single day when you don't do it, you'll sink, you'll hit bottom, and then there won't be any way to come back. Understand?"

"No, yes," I say, confused.

He comes even closer, his face too near mine.

"Pain. That's what you have to provoke."

"Yes."

"Some pain every day, you follow? True pain. In someone you really love. You love your girls?"

I nod, but I still don't know what it is I'm answering.

"That will fill you with guilt, and if the guilt is strong enough, you'll need to stay to take care of them." He squeezes my arm, gazes into my eyes. "Do you want to stay on this side of the world? You want to save them from the damage of losing their mother?"

I feel my feet touching slowly down on the mossy lake bottom, my lungs filling up again with water. I'm just trying to breathe. He watches my expression closely, evaluating me. I wonder if I'll be able to move, if he will release me. I let go of the workbench and I'm still standing. I take a step backward and his hand opens, freeing my arm. I put my hands into my pockets where he can't see them. The guilt will help me, that's what he said. But how? I want to understand exactly how.

I go out into the yard and walk away, tripping twice. Now it's not the man that's scaring me, it's the image of my hands clutching the sliding-door frame, the body that can't hold on, I'm terrified at not knowing how much longer I can hold myself up. The spotlights turn on again. I run to my house, cross the barricade. I go inside with one palm resting on my heart because all I need now is to feel it, but I can't feel anything. Where are my heartbeats? Higher up? Farther in? In the living room I glance around for the rabbit cage but don't see it anywhere. I climb the stairs, biting my lips until they bleed. I walk down the hall, and now I'm in the girls' room. Each in her bed, the cage right between them, empty. There's a movement and I see Blimp tangled in the older one's arms, and I slowly reach out my hands. As soon as the rabbit twitches I press its neck against the mattress. If I loosen my grip its fur starts to slip through my hands. I grab it by the ears the way the man did, and the rabbit's feet are kicking the air. My oldest turns over, but doesn't wake up.

In the kitchen I turn on the lights, pick up a knife, move the faucet to make room, and I put the rabbit inside, pressing it against the sink. I bury the fingers of my free hand into its fur, digging my fingers in around its neck. The rabbit waits, frozen, its red eye on me. I'm thinking about what to do now, how to do it. I'm thinking about how this will spatter the kitchen and I'll have to clean it well, or else the girls will see the disaster first thing in the morning. What if I let it go outside instead of killing it? Will losing it be pain enough? I know it won't be. What if instead of skinning it I squeeze its neck and strangle it, and then I put the dead bunny back into my oldest daughter's arms? If she woke up hugging a dead animal, would that cause her enough pain? Then I understand exactly what guilt does, it enters like the air through the sliding glass door and flows into my lungs. I breathe. The rabbit doesn't even move a whisker. It waits a few seconds, maybe minutes, bearing the pressure of my hands on its body, staring at me and holding so still that in the end we both calm down. I let go and it sits there, frozen, its red unblinking eye on me. I again press the palm of a hand to my chest, and I feel my heart. It's a beautiful beating.

I set the knife aside, turning away from the rabbit in the sink, and it immediately jumps down to the floor and hops away. I leave the kitchen, too—neither of us could bear to stay. When I pass the open glass door, I notice the frame, and now there's no reason to hold on to it. I slide it closed.

In the bathroom, I study my face for a while in the mirror. I sit on the edge of the tub, and then I shower. In the bedroom, my husband is asleep on his side of the bed and I get in carefully, making sure not to move the sheets or shake the mattress. I remember how quickly the exhaustion hits me, how I stretch out my legs, relax my arms alongside my body, and close my eyes. Just a moment before falling asleep, I move my hands and don't feel the sheets. It's just a few seconds, it's the end of falling: the dark and mossy feeling on my fingertips, right when they touch the lake bottom and twitch for one last time.

A FABULOUS ANIMAL

Nearly twenty years after the accident, Elena calls me in Lyon. I don't recognize her voice, but when she says her name, I know exactly who I'm talking to.

For a few seconds, I listen to her breathe. I hold the phone against my ear with my shoulder and light a cigarette. Slowly, trying not to make any noise, I go out to the balcony that overlooks the park, sit down in one of the chairs, and slip off my sandals with my toes. She wants to talk about Peta, her son. She wants to know what I still remember about the night of the accident. Her voice is calm and raspy. I wonder if that's because of the passage of years, or if her sweet voice I remember so well disappeared all at once that last time we saw each other.

I put my bare feet up on the other chair. My heels and legs ache. I was in Madrid this morning and had only just dropped my suitcase in the hallway when the phone rang.

"Where are you, Elena? In Buenos Aires?"

I ask the question to buy time, to arrive home a little more before I surrender to this conversation. Her silence makes me suspect she never left Hurlingham, that she could still be living in the house where it all happened.

"What about you?" asks Elena. "Are you still traveling?"

I think of the new office in Marseille, the urban planning professorship in Barcelona, the commercial development on the outskirts of Bordeaux. But when I picture Elena sitting on the bench in the narrow breezeway between the kitchen and the patio, when I imagine her talking to me from that wooden bench with iron legs that her alcoholic father made with his own two hands as a wedding present and that she would never get rid of, I say, "Yeah, a little," and wait to see what she says.

"I still have your coat."

What coat? There are a dozen coats in my closet now, but I don't remember the ones I used to wear.

"I'm dying, Leila. That's why I'm calling."

I look at my feet and wiggle my toes. Beyond the balcony, the wind caresses the treetops. And then I think of the horse. After all these years I think about it again, about the first time I saw it, and the memory is crushingly clear. I was headed straight from the airport to Elena's house, and the taxi stopped at a light on Avenida Vergara, right beside the animal. It was balking, harnessed to a cart piled high with mattresses, and a man was whipping it to make it walk. There had always been horses in greater Buenos Aires, but I'd been living abroad for some time, and the image was startling.

The horse's belly was so close that I could have reached my hand out of the car window and touched it. It looked swollen, disproportionate to the rest of its skinny body. Bowed legs, hair worn away around the reins. But above all what I remember is how the horse abruptly turned its head and looked at me. It stared straight at me with those big, dark eyes.

"I know it was a long time ago," says Elena, "but . . . remember the costume Peta was wearing that night, the one he'd made himself? I want someone to talk to me about my Peta." When Elena coughs, I get a sense of what has made her voice change so much. "Please, you were there. Who can I ask if not you?"

I wait a few seconds, and when Elena doesn't say anything more I ask, "You're sick? What's wrong?"

"It doesn't matter, Leila. We're over sixty years old, and I won't make it through the next month." There's a slight jump in her voice, as if she'd abruptly stood up. "I've been trying to reach you for a while."

"Are you in Hurlingham?" I ask.

We were both born in Hurlingham, but we met in college, at the school of architecture.

"Yes," says Elena.

I think of Alberto, and now I'm trying not to ask about him.

"But you did move?" I ask instead.

I remember them on the patio, the same patio where the accident happened.

"I'm still in the house." She coughs again. "Hold on a minute."

It sounds like she puts the phone down on the bench and walks away. She leaves me alone in her breezeway, so close to the patio that, in Lyon, the hairs on my arms stand on end.

Alberto and Elena got married a year after they met. All three of us graduated that December, but then I accepted my position at a French firm and left Argentina. I always wrote to them when I was passing through Buenos Aires, and they'd have me over to dinner at their small, middle-class house that they had meticulously redesigned themselves. They were tall and hardy and wore the architect's signature light shirts and pants, with their designer watches a little loose on their wrists. Elena pulled her brown hair back into a ponytail, and the curls around her forehead stuck up like little springs. Sometimes Alberto would push them back behind her ears. It was an affectionate gesture, but he did it mostly when she was the one talking and his attention started to wander.

Over the phone, I hear a refrigerator door open. I remember every detail of that kitchen. The breezeway was only two steps away, practically an extension of the patio, because in the first remodel they'd replaced one wall with a sliding glass door, and it was always open. And there, sitting on the bench, was where Elena liked to "feel the air." The house wasn't big, but they had torn down some dividing walls, and they knew just where to place the lights and armchairs to make it seem spacious. They had their son a couple of years after graduation, and they raised him with the same care and shared devotion with which they took on all their professional projects. At the time of my last visit they'd been married for nine years, and the boy had just turned seven.

Elena gives a little cry, and something hits the floor. *Who will*

I tell about this call? I wonder. No one in France knows about this. Actually, not even Elena knows what happened to me that night, aside from the accident itself. She's calling because she wants to hear someone talk about Peta; as far as she knows, there is nothing else.

Elena's footsteps return, and she picks up the phone. The bench creaks when she sits back down.

"I'm drinking Fernet," she says. "I want to pick up at least one vice before I die. You think I'm in time?"

"Of course," I say. "We can drink six of them over the phone every day."

We laugh. If she really did need it, I'd be willing to keep her company. That's how it always is: I'll suddenly realize how much I miss someone, the anguish hits all at once, and then I have to fight back the tears.

I hear her light a cigarette; I didn't know she smoked. I try to remember some detail about Peta, but all I see is the horse. Elena inhales, and the cigarette paper hisses. She's not going to say anything else until I start talking.

"He was the one who opened the door for me that day."

Elena exhales the smoke slowly, sounding almost relieved.

His name was Pedro, but he went by Peta. I met him when he was two, on the first of a dozen or so visits I made to Buenos Aires after my firm was signed on to develop two high-rises in Puerto Madero. I also saw him one night when he was four, but he was already asleep. And then that time, when he was seven; all the images that come to me now are from that final visit.

I see him standing in the doorway, wrapped in a long makeshift dress of metallic paper, his chest puffed out stiffly like a gendarme's.

I tell Elena how shocked I was to see him so big, and how I always remember the two of them—"you and Alberto," I say—setting out appetizers on the patio, coming and going from the kitchen with that efficient harmony they had in everything they did. I say "did," and then pause to see if she clarifies anything about Alberto. After a few seconds I go on. I describe the house, the big mirror they had just installed in the hall. How tired I was from the trip, and how the first drink on the patio eased everything. It's incredible the things you remember after twenty years have passed. For example, how my feet were bare, and the patio tiles still warm. Maybe it's the feelings of pleasure and pain that always leave a more vivid sensation, because they're things that happen in the body. Or maybe it's because there was a time when I went over those memories a lot, and consciously chose which details I'd return to in order to understand what had happened.

On my balcony, the evening begins to darken.

"I'm going to make myself a drink too, Elena."

"I'll wait."

I leave the phone on my chair, go inside, and cross the two large living rooms to the dining room. I wonder if Elena would feel comfortable among so many bookshelves. Whether she would approve of my armchairs, the big stained-glass window in the open kitchen, the walnut floor that my second ex-husband insisted on installing. I open the small bar cabinet and pour a finger of whiskey. Elena just wants someone to say Peta's name. To describe the way he tied his colorful sneakers, his meticulously messy room, his smooth, short fingernails flecked with paint. Then I have a realization: This might be the last time we ever talk. That's what this call is about, and so, even if all she wants is to hear me talk about Peta, I understand that I'm going to tell her about the horse.

I carry my whiskey back outside while I organize my memories, struck by their clarity as they unfurl in my head.

"You still there?" I ask.

"Yes."

"I don't have kids, Elena. I never had any, but . . . You're going to think this is my own thing, something personal, that it has nothing to do with what happened to Peta."

I wait. Silence was always a symptom of Elena's unease.

I tell her about what I discovered that night after talking with Peta for a while, as we lay side by side on the rug. I already knew about the boy's quirks, and about his talent for drawing. How two years before, when he was five, he had studied the path the daylight took across his bedroom walls, and how he "showed" his artworks by hanging them only in those areas of "real" light. His obsession with painting horses, and his command, at the age of seven, of perspective and color. A lot of parents overestimate their children's talent, and I hadn't known until that moment how much was really going on in Peta's head. Maybe because he was the son of architects, or maybe it was pure talent, but in any case, Peta was truly remarkable.

That night, after the boy went upstairs alone to his room,

Elena and Alberto insisted that I be the one to go up and make sure he brushed his teeth and got into bed. I agreed right away when they laughingly admitted that when they had people over for dinner, once Peta finished eating, he would only answer questions from the guests, and he refused to say a word to his parents. They thought it was his way of inviting new people to his room. I accepted the challenge, and as soon as I was alone with the boy, I asked him why he did what he did. Peta said, "I pretend they're dead," and he laughed with a hand over his mouth, seduced by his own game. He invited me to stretch out on the rug so he could show me his ceiling, and he pointed to the constellations he'd been marking with a hole punch, chipping away at the paint. They were barely perceptible from the floor, because he was only working on the marks; he planned to paint them in time for Elena's next birthday. I asked him how he reached the ceiling on his own, and he said, "I have a method," but didn't say what it was. We stayed there for a while, lying belly-up, until he turned to me, very serious, and asked, "Have you ever woken up in the middle of the night? I mean without anyone waking you up—have you ever woken up for real?"

He was an extraordinary kid, and at the same time an extremely normal one. Actually, the only extraordinary thing until that moment was happening inside me: There, lying on the rug next to him, I fantasized about the idea that someone could need me so specifically, so exclusively. And yet, I didn't want to be a mother, I'd never been interested until then.

I don't say anything about this to Elena, about how Peta

asked me questions and I thought, *What he is asking seems simple, but it's actually quite complex;* I thought, *Do the adults around this child understand the magnitude of this question?* I thought, *I can understand it, I can answer without misleading or destroying him.* It was a powerful intuition, an impulse that told me: this boy is a precious thing, and *you* would be capable of caring for something like him.

I tell her only what Peta said next: "I don't want to be an architect." I don't mention what I thought: that the firm tone of his voice, the way his eyes shone as he discovered the meaning of his words, seemed also to suggest, *I am such a majestic being that I cannot allow myself the world of men.* Nor do I tell her that I waited a few calculated seconds before speaking again, in order to give Peta time to fully savor his own discovery and recognize it in all its splendor, nor that I nodded at him as if to say, *Yes! Yes! That is the real truth! You can be whatever you want!*

I tell Elena only what I asked Peta then.

"And what do you want to be?"

"I want to be a horse."

"A horse?" Elena's voice trembles over the phone.

I tell her that I leapt up from the floor and proposed to Peta that we practice.

"Practice being horses?" he asked. "How do you do that?"

"However you think."

Peta also leapt to his feet. The certainty of my answer seemed to fill him with energy.

"You practice being a horse by walking with one foot right in front of the other," he said.

"Great! Let's practice!"

We walked in a line side by side, from one end of the room to the other, back and forth, our arms outstretched and our hands open, pretending we were making a great effort not to lose our balance.

"And the more you close your eyes, the more you're a horse," said Peta.

"Great!"

We closed our eyes and practiced another round back and forth.

"And the higher you are . . . ," Peta said, jumping onto the edge of the bed, "the more horse you are."

He put one foot in front of the other on the wooden footboard and tried to walk with his eyes closed.

Elena makes a noise over the phone, confused and guttural, as if she had swallowed something full of pain, and I know she is thinking of the ledge over the patio.

"When you left the room, was he in bed?"

I don't remember, but I say he was. We fall silent, and I don't know whether I should go on.

"Oh, Leila." I hear the paper of her cigarette spark. "No matter how much it hurts, whatever you tell me about Peta is like being with him for a few more seconds. Thank you."

"There's more. Something I want to tell you."

I think of the patio where Peta had played from the time he started to crawl, Elena sitting on the bench in the breezeway, always close, always attentive. She read, worked, talked on the phone, always with one eye on Peta. Sometimes she leaned her head against the wall and closed her eyes, but didn't sleep. I remember the mark on the ivory wallpaper right at the height of her head, like a hazy cloud. Will she die sitting there? Is there something I could do to get her up off that bench? Get her up for what?

"When Peta fell from the ledge . . . ," I begin, but then I stop short.

I gaze out at the park beyond the balcony: night has fallen in Lyon.

And suddenly all the words are there, and I start saying them into the phone. I can no longer tell what is logical or illogical, what might be painful and what might be bearable. I relate what happened just as I remember it: the sound of the body hitting the patio tiles. How it took all three of us a moment to understand, to turn around at the table and react. How, finally, the two of them jumped up from their chairs and ran to Peta. Alberto didn't want to move him, Elena picked him up and pressed him to her body, and she wanted to cry out but couldn't, because neither she nor the boy was breathing. Elena was kneeling and the blood pooled out around her, and it seemed like the whole problem was that she was squeezing her son too tightly. I remember I got up from the table and said, "I'll call an ambulance," but no one said anything or moved. I remember I ran to the kitchen and called. I gave the address, answered some questions, and when I hung up, I couldn't go back to the patio. My coat was on the breezeway bench, and that's where I left it. I walked out of the house. I closed the front door behind me, and the click of the latch confirmed that

I was now on the other side. I stood staring down at the knob, and I heard Elena scream. And then, without turning around, I sensed something strange happening behind me. I couldn't bring myself to turn around and see. Some drops of sweat rolled from my forehead to my chin and fell onto the flagstone. *Turn around,* I told myself, *the worst of the pain is in the house.* Elena was still screaming. *Whatever happens now, it's not going to kill you,* I thought. And I turned toward the street.

Lying on the pavement, under the faint light from the only streetlamp at the end of the block, the body was so big and disproportionate that at first I didn't understand what it was. It was a horse, lying in the road as if fallen from above. I approached slowly, trying not to scare it. It was panting, the swollen stomach rising and falling, stretching out the hide worn away by the reins. Its big dark eyes were searching the night, and I felt certain they were searching for me. It raised its head to look straight at me. It snorted, tried to get up, but couldn't. I knelt beside it, hugged its head, and pressed my face against its forelock. "You're going to be okay," I said. "Easy now."

First the ambulance arrived, then the police. Without getting up I directed them toward the house. Soon, neighbors started appearing. They came up, saw the horse, and stood there, baffled. And the whole time I stayed right where I was, my arms around the animal.

Some minutes later I saw Alberto and Elena come out behind a stretcher. Behind me, a neighbor was calling an emergency veterinarian. Something caught Elena's attention and she looked toward me, confused. Then she stumbled into the ambulance, the EMTs slammed the doors shut, and the siren's shrill noise sped away.

I'm quiet for a moment. I move the phone away from my ear and breathe deeply. A few seconds later I ask her:

"Do you remember the horse?"

Elena says nothing.

There was a wake three days later, and then a burial. Before I left I hugged each of them, first Alberto, then Elena, separate for the first time, motionless among the guests, attentive, but in a strange way: to the floor, to the smallest of sounds, searching amid the turmoil for something they seemed to have had in their hands just a second ago.

I took care of the horse. It spent several days recovering in a university animal hospital. I found some stables in Luján, where they gave me a good deal if I paid for the year up front. I was willing to spend a fortune on it, but two weeks later someone called me in Lyon to tell me that a man had claimed the horse, and the animal was back with its owner. I think it was in those days when I called Hurlingham to see how they were, but they didn't answer. Or maybe I meant to call, and in the end I didn't. They didn't call me either. And we never spoke again.

I hear a creaking sound over the phone, the bench's legs scraping. Did Elena stand up? Is she gazing at the patio? What is the patio like now? Why doesn't she say anything?

"Elena, are you there?"

Sometimes I dream I'm back in Buenos Aires. I'm almost

always in a taxi, staring out the window. And then I see it. I recognize it immediately. Its color, height, its ears. It's struggling to pull a cart. An enormous cart, disproportionate to the horse's size. I ask the taxi driver to stop, and I get out and run to it. The man whipping it doesn't understand what is happening, and he pulls on the reins to halt the animal. The horse stops, snorts, turns to me. I touch his big head, my forehead against his once again. One open palm against his cheek, the other on his shoulder. He is so enormous and beautiful, and I am asking for his forgiveness.

"Leila, I don't have time to waste, don't you realize that?"

She's right, she's so right. What are we going to do now?

"It's over," she says, but there is a subtle change in her energy. "Where is he?"

I hold the phone, trying to put myself in her place. What is she asking me?

"The horse, Leila."

"The horse," I say, buying time, trying to understand this last request. I search desperately among my memories of Argentina, trying to come up with a place where there is a horse, any horse, that can be hugged.

"Leila . . ."

"Right," I say. "Let's see, do you have a pen?"

"I do," she says, and I hear a noise I recognize clearly: she pushes the glass door open. The sound changes completely. Elena is standing in front of the patio. "I have everything," she says. "All ready here. I'm listening."

WILLIAM IN THE WINDOW

I went to Shanghai a few months after we got the news of his illness, and shortly before his treatment started. I called him every other night and he answered in his morning, making coffee or just finishing it, and he'd ask how my book was coming along.

I was writing a novel about a woman who goes back to work two years after having a baby; her daughter grows furious at her disappearance and rejects her. The father steps in and starts taking care of the little girl, and if the woman ever dares to approach her, the baby starts to scream as if she were being stabbed. I updated Andrés on my progress with the novel, but I also said, *This is going to take longer than I thought,* or even, *I have to rewrite the whole fourth chapter,* and once I went so far as to say, *There's a problem with the narrator, I have to start all over again.*

Sometimes we went a few seconds without saying anything, and I could hear the sound of his lips sipping coffee.

"I just want it to be perfect," I would say.

"All right," he'd say, "take all the time in the world."

But what I heard was, *I'm waiting for you,* and also, *Why aren't you here right now?*

The only thing I had done conscientiously in Buenos Aires, before deciding to take the trip, was wait in horror for the moment when I would find him dead. When I'd come home and see him stiff on the sofa, or turn over at night in bed and brush his leg with my foot and feel his cold, rigid skin. I was frightened by the idea of his dead body, the entirety of his physical part there in the house, totally emptied of him. But above all I was frightened by the suspicion that if Andrés died, I might die with him.

"And today?" Andrés would ask. "How did the writing go today?"

More than once I got the impression that in his interpretation of my book, the mother was my alter ego, and he was the father taking care of the little girl. After all, they had both been left at home, the two of them alone and in charge of the most problematic thing. But the woman's story was based on my sister, who had three kids and two husbands and dealt with them all in well-organized shifts. It seemed like, more than a family, she ran an office of state employees, and her entire job consisted of understanding priorities and delegating responsibilities to people she would have preferred to fire. If I asked Andrés about my sister, he inevitably had something to say, because on Thursdays we always used to babysit her twins together, and now that I wasn't there, Andrés still had them over and still watched them. He told me about what they had done, what they'd eaten, and what games they had invented.

"All right," I'd say.

I used it too, that *all right.* But mine was a concession, a silence, a *go on.*

The Shanghai Writers' Association had given me a room on the forty-second floor of a skyscraper that overlooked Zhongshan Park. When I talked to Andrés, I sat on the windowsill and gazed out at the illuminated city on the other side of the glass. He had googled the streets around my building and found a Carrefour just two blocks away, plus a café selling the kind of croissants I liked, and a zoo that even he would have been interested in visiting.

"Although you'd have to take the subway there," he said. "I guess you won't want to get that far away from work, right?"

I put up my feet, leaning against the window frame and hugging my knees, my forehead pressed against the pane. Bouquets of skyscrapers scattered in both directions along the horizon. From miles away I could see the lights of elevators going up and down, while he said, *Meat is still getting more expensive here,* or maybe, *I found the sewing scissors you lost, guess where you left them.*

In the mornings I went to the national library and spent a couple of hours working there in the main hall. It was one of the few areas where people didn't use the library as a dining hall. I would have preferred to write in peace at my little apartment, but it was only twenty-three square meters, including the bathroom with a washer and the foyer that doubled as a kitchen. Maybe it was big enough for one person's life, but there was no work desk, and the tiny breakfast table was terribly uncomfortable and unstable. I didn't leave mugs or cups on it because I was afraid I would knock them over when I walked by, brushing against it on the way to the bathroom or back to the bedroom.

The other nine guests of the residency, all foreign writers, lived in identical apartments distributed throughout other floors of the building. We had gathered all together twice, first at the welcome cocktail hour and then at an interminable day of association readings, where our contributions were interspersed with those of fifty-two Chinese writers, with short breaks to drink tea and eat lunch.

I met Mega and Gonçalo at that reading, while we were in line for coffee. Mega was Indian and my age. Gonçalo was Portuguese but lived in Madrid; he was tall and handsome, with eyes that would turn to your breasts the second you broke eye contact. The three of us spoke English together and mine was pretty bad, but there was no one else to talk to, so we spent the whole break together.

It was at lunch on that same day, finally seated before a regiment of tables piled with food, when I met Denyse. She was Irish and about my mother's age. She had short hair and wore a pair of white earrings. She wasn't really that skinny, but her limbs were so slender that she looked it. Her hands and wrists, even her ears—everything seemed fragile and delicate. She had started writing novels later in life. She'd done very well with the first one, which she had based on a Serbian woman who cleaned her house. This woman had been nine years old during the Belgrade bombings in the nineties, and apparently she'd spent four of the roughest months hidden in a windowless room with two other kids, writing, in shifts and on the pages of a large accounting book, an etiquette manual on how to drink tea. The woman still had a few pages of that manual, which they printed in facsimile at the end of Denyse's novel, along with a photo of Denyse and her Serbian maid in the town where they both still lived, two hours outside of Dublin. Later, Denyse had written two more novels, but they hadn't done as well. Her son, Henry, who was what had given her the most work in her life, had moved out by then, but she still had a husband and a cat, and she found it hard to write at home. Her editor had gotten her this residency so she could work on a sequel to that first novel. I told her about my own novel with the screaming little girl, about the Boedo neighborhood where I lived in Buenos Aires, and about Andrés, though I didn't mention his illness. Some days later we met up for coffee, and another night we had dinner at a Chinese-French fusion restaurant a hundred and seven floors up, where they brought you the menu in a dozen languages.

A few mornings after that, I was heading down to buy coffee and ran into Denyse on the elevator. Her face was so red that it took me a few seconds to recognize her—she had been crying since early morning. I convinced her to sit down on the building's front steps, where she was silent for a while before she found the strength to tell me what had happened. Her fourteen-year-old cat, William, had spent the night at the veterinarian's. It wasn't until a few hours ago that he had started to show signs of recovery.

"I do love my husband," she said. "It's not that I don't love him. But William is all I have."

She seemed so upset I thought it best not to ask any questions. We went to Carrefour and bought Milka chocolate, water crackers, sliced bread, and coffee. We paid three times what those products cost at home, but we knew they would be good consolation, and by the time we got back, Denyse was feeling a little calmer.

Two weeks later, William was better. The veterinarian said he'd been poisoned, and for the past ten days her husband had come straight home from work to be sure William was still on the mend, and then headed out to go from house to house ringing doorbells and talking to the neighbors. The husband's name was Brian, and Brian was sure that if the man who had poisoned William opened the door to him, he would be capable of spotting his hatred immediately. Brian was willing to talk it over, to hear out reasons, analyze misunderstandings, whatever was necessary to make peace.

"That's the man I married," said Denyse. "At first you think he's a hero, after ten years he's more like a sucker, after twenty he's a blockhead, and by then it's too late to break up."

I asked if she thought he'd be able to find the poisoner.

"The thing is that if he doesn't, this could happen again," she said.

We were taking a short walk through the roses of Zhongshan Park, and we sat down for a moment across from one of the gardens.

"I'm not one of those women who are afraid of getting divorced," she said. "If that was what I wanted, I would do it immediately."

I hadn't asked her anything, so I didn't reply either.

"But the cat is his. And I can't live without the cat."

That was the only time she called him "the cat," and not "William."

I told Andrés the whole story, and by the next time we talked, he had googled Denyse and found a photo of Brian. An interview in a local paper said that the Serbian cleaning woman still worked for them, and there was even a photo of their house in Kilkenny. In the image, William was sitting in the window. Andrés sent me the link, and I sat staring at the cat for a while. His ear closest to the camera was perked up and alert; William seemed to know that the photographer was there, but, stoic and dignified, had decided to ignore him and stare off in another direction.

Denyse had started taking notes for the sequel to her novel, and I had progressed another three chapters in mine. My character was still mired in her ordeal. She came home from work and the little girl wouldn't even let her get close enough for a kiss. At bedtime, only the father could take her up to her room, get her PJs on, and tuck her in. If the mother dared to peek in at them, even just to wave good night, the girl started shrieking in pure rage. The neighbors, worried by the endless screaming, had knocked at the door to find out what was going on; later, still suspicious, they'd called the police, so that one night, the mother found herself obliged to sit in her kitchen for two hours answering questions from a child abuse specialist.

"Do you think it's her fault?" asked Andrés. "Is she a woman who doesn't love her baby?"

"But she's not doing anything to her!"

"Tomorrow the doctors are going to repeat the tests," he said.

This was two nights before what happened with Denyse.

"How long does it take to get the results?"

"Six working days."

"All right" was what I said. *All right.*

After that we had an excursion with the full group, the ten foreign writers plus seven association employees. They took us to Wuzhen by bus. I sat with Mega, the Indian writer, who told me that she'd slept with Gonçalo but it hadn't gone anywhere. Now every time she ran into him he was with a different Chinese girl, and the few times he was alone he'd tell her, *But I do miss you, I was really moved by what happened between us.* He sat two seats ahead of us and occasionally turned around and smiled, looking apologetic. Denyse sat with Alan, an Australian around her age who wrote detective novels, probably the only one of us who actually wrote more than two thousand words a day and made a living from his books. After the tour, lunch, and a meet-and-greet with authorities, we had a free hour before heading back, and Denyse and I sat down by one of the canals to have a cup of coffee together.

Denyse was a good conversationalist and didn't mind silences; something about her calmness felt soothing. I also liked that she rolled up her shirtsleeves the same way my mother did. Then I heaved a sigh, and I told her. I don't know why, maybe because I had no one else to tell. That Andrés was sick, and what I was most afraid of in the world was his death, because if he died, I might die with him. I thought of the photo of William in the window in Kilkenny, gazing haughtily off to the side, and the way in which, a few days ago, Denyse had told me that the cat was Brian's, but that she couldn't live without the cat. And Denyse put her hand around her mug but didn't pick it up. She kept holding it like that, as if it could take off flying any second.

"What are the things you like about him?" she asked after a while.

It was a tough question, but I thought that the correct answer would help her give me advice. I thought about it carefully and came up with something small, almost funny, but sincere.

"When he goes to the bathroom," I said, "to our bathroom in Buenos Aires, you can see that he stands in front of the toilet, and when he pees, he rests one hand on the tiles."

Denyse looked at me and nodded, then finally let go of the mug.

"He has strong, manly hands, with long fingers and square palms. I like that blurry mark he leaves of himself. It moves me somehow."

It made me happy to see that the mark was always there, always a recent, renewed impression. And also that it was something only I could see, even if it was just at a certain time of day when the light was exactly right.

"It's something that he does for me every day," I said, "even if he has no idea he's doing it."

Denyse nodded again. My heart was pounding, but I had no idea why.

Later, when I sat on the windowsill and spoke to Andrés, I almost told him what I'd said to Denyse. My forehead was pressed against the cold glass, and I wanted to tell him I missed him. Something new and painful had settled into my chest. If that impulse was the urgent need for him to be near, then everything could be put right again: I had only to return to Buenos Aires on the first plane the next day. But he was talking about the twins, and I said yes, I said *all right.* And that was the last time we spoke before the thing I want to talk about happened.

Denyse had gotten the internal numbers of all the resident writers and was calling us one by one. It was her birthday, and she wanted to invite us over for mac and cheese in her room.

"How do we do it?" I liked the idea and wanted to help, but I still didn't understand the plan. "All of us having dinner in your room? We don't even have enough plates!"

Denyse said it would be like in the old days at college. Everyone would bring their own dishes and silverware, the stools we all had in our bathrooms, and their own beers. She would go to Carrefour and buy ten frozen macaroni and cheese dinners and something for dessert. All we'd have to do was heat them up two by two in the little microwave. She would get a plastic tablecloth to put over the mattress and we'd sit around the bed.

"Do you think it's childish?" she asked.

"I think it's great," I said. "Don't buy dessert, I'll bring a cake and a candle."

She agreed immediately. I went down to a little bakery I'd seen in the subway station right across from our building where they sold fancy chocolate cakes, and I chose one for her. We all arrived right on time. Mega and Gonçalo knocked at the door together, but they barely exchanged a single word all evening. Alan brought a small bouquet of flowers that Denyse put in a vase and set on the windowsill. We all handed over our dishes in the hallway-kitchen, put our cans of beer in the freezer, which was soon full, and carried our stools into the bedroom to choose a spot around the bed and settle in as best we could.

"Why didn't we do this sooner!" the Danish poet exclaimed several times.

The Slovenian writer, who was a lot older and couldn't figure out how to sit comfortably on her stool, excused herself and left as soon as we finished the mac and cheese. But the rest of us were content, laughing and continuously switching up our conversation partners, happy to finally be able to share discoveries and anecdotes from our experiences in Shanghai. Sometimes a comment caught people's attention and the silence of good stories fell over us, and every once in a while someone got up and went to the freezer for another round of cold beers. I think we'd all gone a long time without being part of a spontaneous gathering with more than one or two other people, and I was happy to see Denyse having fun, offering seconds with a big smile, and asking for requests for music, which played pleasantly in the background.

I was telling Alan about the problem of Chinese fishing boats in the Argentine ocean when the Korean writer started talking about how her aunt had killed her sister—that is, the Korean writer's mother—in a domestic accident. The particulars were so suspicious, the details so sinister, that we all started listening closely. Absorbed in a description of the small detached kitchen where it had all happened, no one noticed Denyse get up from her stool and walk off toward the kitchen area. Then I saw Gonçalo looking her way with a confused expression, and followed his eyes to see Denyse leaning against the hallway counter, staring at the floor. I leapt up and the group gradually fell silent, trying to figure out what was happening. I went over to Denyse, and when she didn't react I took her hands; her phone was in her right one.

"Brian called," she said. "William is dead."

I waited to see what else she would say, but she was quiet, so I hugged her. She pressed her face into my hair and said: "He was poisoned again."

I thought about Brian, about how evidently he hadn't found the culprit in time. Mega came over too, and then Alan. Someone turned off the music. I explained who William was, and Brian, and what had happened, while the rest of the guests started to stand up. Denyse was shaking and we all exchanged glances—no one knew her well enough to tell whether it was better to stay and keep her company or leave her alone. I started to gather up plastic mac and cheese trays, used napkins, and other trash from dinner, and carried everything to the hallway-kitchen. The group followed my lead. We threw out the empty beer cans, and each guest spontaneously picked up their dishes and stool and said goodbye to the others, saving their last hugs for Denyse, who accepted them a little dazed, unable to say much. Alan was the last to go, and then I offered to stay with her. She roundly refused.

"I need to be alone," she said.

I understood, because I would have wanted the same thing. I reminded her that she still had the chocolate cake in her fridge, and that it could be a good consolation when she needed it. And I was only a few floors up, ready to come down and make coffee at any hour. She insisted she was okay, that she needed to cry in peace, and that we would talk tomorrow. She left me in the hallway with the two bags of trash, and closed the door.

Back in my room, I brushed my teeth, put on my pajamas, and sat in bed to jot down some ideas for my novel before I forgot them. The mother would figure out that if she crawled around and meowed like a kitten, then her little girl would accept her. She would spend almost half a year like that, crawling around the house and eating dinner from a plate on the floor, all so the girl would first start to scratch her behind the ears, then accept a kiss, and finally the woman would manage to stand up without being bombarded by shrieks.

I was getting into bed, about to turn out the light, when the landline phone rang. *Must be Denyse,* I thought, and reached toward the nightstand to answer.

"I need you to come down here," she said, and hung up.

It was like a thriller—short, concise, with that definitive clincher of the line going dead, so dramatic that I sat staring at the phone, disconcerted. After a few seconds I got moving, thinking she must just be upset, and I pictured myself making coffee and cutting two generous slices of cake. Maybe it would even be a good anecdote to look back on years later, because Denyse's friendship already seemed like the kind that comes unexpectedly, but then turns out to be lifelong. I donned a coat over my pajamas and put on a pair of slippers, then headed back to her apartment.

I knocked at the door and heard Denyse's voice tell me to come in. I found her in the hallway, sitting on the floor with her back against the refrigerator cabinet. I thought that no matter how much Denyse had loved the cat, surely she had been through much more harrowing things, and I was pained to see her so caught up in this other kind of suffering. I sat down beside her, shoulder to shoulder, and stayed there for a while without saying anything. She wasn't crying—I got the feeling she still wasn't ready to cry.

"I never imagined myself saying something like this," she said, "but I have to say it."

I almost said *all right,* because what else could I say? I didn't have the slightest idea what she was talking about.

"William is in the apartment."

"In what apartment?"

"Here."

I waited, in case I had misunderstood.

"I can hear him," she said.

It's fine, I thought. *She's in shock.* I decided I would make that coffee and I started to get up, but she grabbed my wrist and stopped me.

"I am rational and mature enough to understand that this cannot be happening." She spoke precisely, seriously. "But if I'm going crazy, I need someone to stay with me."

I nodded.

"Because you don't hear it, do you?"

Before answering, out of respect, I listened for a few seconds to the silence in the room. Then I shook my head.

"But what is it that you hear?" I asked. "A meow?"

"His scratching."

She raised a finger, but since she couldn't point to any particular place she ended up resting it on her lips.

"There. Hear it?"

I shook my head.

"William digs his claws in slowly, like this, it's his way. On my pillow, for example, when I'm about to fall asleep. There it is again!"

Again, I shook my head.

"Crackling, like those bags with little plastic bubbles that are so fun to pop. It's him! Are you sure you don't hear it?"

I said no again and we sat in silence for a moment. I tried to really pay attention, because maybe there was another noise that, in her desperation, she was associating with William. But I didn't hear a thing.

"How about I make some coffee?" I offered.

"Has this ever happened to you? Have you ever gone a little crazy?"

I got up and she didn't stop me. I knew from my own apartment where the little electric coffeemaker was and how to use it, and I found a packet of coffee on the counter. I thought about her question—*had* I ever felt like that? I turned on the faucet. I wanted to think of an example, but couldn't come up with anything.

"Did you talk to Brian again?"

"We exchanged some messages. I don't think he's ready to talk. He must feel guilty for not figuring out who did it."

I filled the filter with coffee and pressed the red button.

Then I heard it. Clear and crackling, a slow scratch over soft fabric, like hundreds of tiny bubbles exploding in the air. I froze with the two coffee cups in my hand, my head turning side to side like a real crazy person. Denyse jumped to her feet.

"William," she said. "You hear him too."

"Yes."

My heart was pounding just like it had when I'd told Denyse about the mark Andrés left in the bathroom. What if William really was in the room with us? And what if the mark had never been there, and I'd only imagined it? And what if Denyse had made it all up and there was no cat or son or husband? What if Andrés was already dead but no one had been able to reach me? What if I was crazy too, and I was losing all control over my life? What if I really did die when Andrés died, but alone and twelve thousand miles away?

I felt Denyse's hand on mine. She was standing in front of me, and she took the mugs and set them on the counter. The coffee was starting to percolate, and she switched it off so nothing would drown out William's call. I felt a cold, prickling fear. When the scratching sound came again, Denyse let out a shriek. Now that I heard it too, she was just as scared as I was. We walked together toward the bedroom, where we looked at the walls and held hands. Two more scratches, long and powerful, seemed to climb up to the ceiling and move toward the door. Now the sound was in the hallway, so we stayed frozen where we were, staring toward the kitchen with the backs of our legs touching the edge of the bed.

"Should we call Alan?" I asked. "Or Mega?"

Denyse shook her head.

"Brian?"

I thought of Andrés and was alarmed that I ruled him out immediately, even though he was the only one out of all of them who would be awake at that hour and would surely answer the phone.

"If William is here," Denyse said, dropping onto the bed, "he has something to tell me."

I sat down next to her. She was mechanically stroking my hand, almost seeming to dig in her nails, her eyes fixed on some point of that narrow hallway on the thirty-ninth floor of that Shanghai building, where suddenly the world had opened into a new dimension.

"This is how everything I don't understand feels," she said. "Like the night Henry was born and it was two minutes and three seconds before he took his first breath. Like this, exactly like this."

I felt a heart pounding in my ears, but was it mine or was it hers?

"Madness scares you, it distracts you, but you have to look at it closely."

The scratching came down from the ceiling to the kitchen counter, and Denyse closed her eyes. She murmured quietly to herself while the sound began moving back toward us. Right when she opened her eyes, it stopped. Now we were both staring in the same direction, toward the place the sound seemed to have entered: the small white refrigerator, its own automated heart galloping at full speed to keep the few remaining beers cold in its minuscule freezer. I jumped up and opened the door, and when I knelt down the chill hit my face. Only one can was still standing; the other five, toppled over and exploded, were bubbling desperately.

I pointed to them, and Denyse approached fearfully, but relaxed as soon as she saw the beers. I wondered if I needed to explain anything, but I saw in her slumped shoulders, in her suddenly exhausted expression, that she understood.

She nodded, and I nodded too, relieved.

"He's gone," she said.

I emptied the freezer and took the beer cans with me. By the time I gave her one last hug, Denyse had finally started to cry.

Back in my apartment, I turned on all the lights and opened my own freezer. I wanted to see what was in there, and I was reassured to find it empty. I sat on the windowsill and called

Andrés to tell him what had happened. It took him a minute to calm down and stop asking questions—he was scared by how late I was calling, and how I wouldn't stop talking about Denyse. He asked me several times if I was okay, if there wasn't really something else that I needed to tell him. "That's it," I said.

"All right."

And then I realized that no, that wasn't it. I was holding back the most important thing. That the cat was dead, but Denyse was still alive.

"She's going to survive," I said.

"Of course."

And it's hard to explain how, but this is really the strangest thing that happened that summer in Shanghai. At some point in the conversation I had left the window. I had peeled my head from the glass, my whole body away from that night that lay between us, and now I was standing in the apartment's little bathroom, holding the phone to my ear, right in front of the toilet.

"What's wrong?" asked Andrés.

I wanted to tell him again that nothing was wrong, everything was fine, and that I would be on a flight back the next day. But I was staring at the mark, the impression of his open palm on the tiles, his daily offering that was just for me, now from the other side of the world. The noise resounded in my ears, crackling like bubbles all around me. And then I saw him. William in the Kilkenny window, upright and attentive, finally turning toward me, recognizing me, granting me the certainty of his gaze.

AN EYE IN THE THROAT

My father picks up the phone. He is twenty-seven years old, and, as everyone does in the nineties, he picks up the receiver without knowing who is calling. People phone and say, "It's Carmen" or "I'm from the post office" or "Hello, I'd like to confirm your appointment." But at night, if the phone rings and my father picks up, no one answers. He waits with the receiver to his ear until he gets tired of standing there doing nothing, or asking questions in vain, or sometimes even cursing. He lowers the receiver onto its base, and though the mechanical click puts an end to the session, he senses there is something more. The silence that calls him every night sticks with him throughout the day, and he can't help but think about Morris. About Morris and the three gas pump islands at the service station in General Acha, about the eighteen hoses hanging from their handles, about the nocturnal lights of that YPF station on the side of the flat, endless highway through the pampa. For my father, the silence is a slippery frustration; the calls, a long enigma that will follow him for nearly twenty years.

It's a time when there are a few household appliances that can function without cords. Hidden inside the battery, the battery hidden in turn inside little plastic compartments, lithium is an imperceptible, encapsulated element silently beating in hundreds and thousands of metal hearts to which no one is paying as much attention as they should. People forget about them, and without the battery in view, in that neighborhood of El Bolsón, Argentina, and in all the cities of the world, this new shape of energy seems like a simple miracle.

To keep the phone from ringing while we're asleep, my father unplugs it before going to bed and plugs it in again the next day. The whole family jealously guards my sleep, and so do the doctors and the woman who comes to clean. "Did the boy sleep well?" they all ask. Sleeping is dangerous. It relaxes my open pharynx, my still-weak muscles, tendons that never healed. If I choke, I wake up. But what is it, really, that chokes me?

Sometimes my mother picks up and the call cuts off immediately. If for some reason my father forgets to disconnect the phone and it rings, we know it rings only for him. And my father, who is a salesman and whose job consists above all of reading things on people's faces that they don't know are written there, stands for a long time with the receiver to his ear, listening to that faceless silence, terrified by his own disquiet.

Almost six months before the calls begin, I am two years old and I'm sitting in front of a Grundig TV screen in my paternal grandmother's living room. When I get distracted, I crawl and toddle around, investigating every object that lies in my path, touching everything my hands can reach. To whomever is put in charge of me, my mother says, "Please pay attention." She had even said it to my father that afternoon, twice, before dropping us off at Grandma's house. Cartoons are on in the living room and they entertain me only sporadically. In the dining room, my father chats with Grandma, keeping constant watch over what I am doing, always attentive to my movements, my constant conversation with the things that surround me.

If I don't clearly understand an object's purpose, I suck it, I bite it, I bang it against another thing. The slippers against the remote control, the remote control against the calculator on the shelf; Grandma's little clock, into my mouth, and then, before I drop it on the floor, I hit it a couple of times on the rug. I am soothed by the objects whose function I can identify. The Russian dolls on the lowest shelf come apart, they go one inside the other and close up again. It's complicated to fit the pieces together, but there is a kind of urge toward completeness in those shapes that can split in two and then come together again, and it fascinates me even more than the digital numbers on the calculator, or the Grundig screen.

All it takes is a long silence for my father to turn around. As I sit in front of the TV surrounded by objects scattered over the floor, I discover that he is afraid. He stands up and rushes over to me, because what is happening is not a tantrum, he understands that right away. This is not the silence that precedes crying. He has seen my face, my cheeks puffed out and turning red—something is happening. It takes him a few more seconds to understand that I'm choking, that I can't breathe. I clench one of my little hands into a fist and clumsily hit at my mouth.

"What did you do?" he asks.

He tries to open my fist, my mouth. I slip away, he catches me. He forces my fingers open. Suddenly I swallow, I swallow something, and my father looks at me in terror.

"What is that? What did you swallow?"

My eyes fill with tears.

"What did you swallow?"

"Nothing," I say.

My voice is so sweet it sounds sincere, and the memory of it interrupts everything each time it comes back to me. A sound that belongs to me but is broken. Action and consequence, scene after scene, from now on my father and I remember everything with the sharpness of an alarm that neither of us will be able to turn off again. I say, "Nothing," and I'm moved by the miracle of my tongue touching my upper palate, the air rushing down my windpipe into my lungs, my vibrating vocal cords.

My father grabs me and I let him; I still trust him. He opens my mouth because he wants to see inside, he wants to believe there is nothing, not now or a moment ago, but he has to be sure.

"Tell me the truth, it's important," he says. "Did you swallow something?"

I shake my head.

"You didn't swallow anything?"

It seems like a different question, but I catch on to the trick and give the same reply.

In El Bolsón and all the cities of the world, in this era when nearly all devices are connected to walls by cords, there is nowhere we can call to reach Mom. If we want to know her opinion, we have to wait for her to return. My father thinks, *He's okay, he's okay,* and it's a silent mantra pounding at his temple from within. Sitting but falling apart, exhausted from so much imagining the worst, he is reassured to see how I get distracted again, how I play and laugh and accept the tangerine wedge he sets in front of me, how I put it in my mouth and swallow and it's fine.

Only in the evening, back at home and after dinner, I start to cough. Later, lying in bed, I wake up retching, and just in case—"It could be anything," says my mother, and, *Better safe than sorry,* thinks my father—they take me to the emergency room. A doctor listens to my chest. "Everything seems all right," he says, smiling at me sympathetically. "Come back later if there are any symptoms." He pinches my cheek. "Or tomorrow, if nothing comes out in his stool but he's still retching." The doctor is already at his office door and scanning the waiting room for his next patient.

Using a fork, Mom conscientiously crushes each bowel movement. She examines me as she saw the doctor do, but with her ears instead of a stethoscope. I squeal with delight at the tickle of that cold ear on my belly, chest, and back, but between peals of laughter I'm still coughing. Mom, who has learned that taking care of someone means understanding what to do and why, listens and listens but doesn't know what she's listening for. She gets restless. She needs a second opinion. We wait until the next day to see the family doctor, and the next day Mom hears the same diagnosis.

On the morning of the third day, I wake up without a voice and with a slight fever, and in the afternoon my breathing trouble starts. Mom calls the hospital, and this time the doctors are alarmed. I vomit in the waiting room and I'm whisked straight to radiology. A doctor hangs the X-ray on a luminous box in front of Mom. The film is a dense black that faintly shows the thoracic bones and the shadows of some organs. In the center, suspended between the clavicles, is a perfect white circle, so brilliant that the light from the box pulsates there. The doctor points with concern to that flash, just below my throat: small, flat, round. My father can't stop recalling it when, after dropping Mom and me off at home, he goes to Grandma's house and checks all the objects I had been playing with. He opens and closes the digital clock on the shelf, opens and closes the battery compartment of the Grundig remote control, opens, but doesn't close, the digital calculator's small black cover. "How did you know it wasn't working?" asks my grandmother, before she quickly connects the dots and understands why her son is standing there but cannot answer her.

Over the phone, they schedule an operation for the next day in Bariloche, seventy-five miles away from El Bolsón. We start off at dawn so as to be at the hospital first thing in the morning. Once I'm checked in, there are a few minutes when I am left alone, when the charge nurse notices that my medical charts are missing and goes back to get them. It might be the first time I've ever been alone in a place that isn't my bedroom or my grandmother's room. I am lying on a gurney in the surgical department's hallway. I'm not scared. I stare up at the fluorescent light on the ceiling, so spectacularly long and flickering. I am aware that I have hardly spoken for a few days now, but what do I know about what is normal and what is not? Yesterday, there was a boy on TV who said that there are false teeth that have to fall out so the real ones can come in; maybe you also stop talking before the first truly adult words come in. Maybe every child my age passes or has passed through a similar hallway, and maybe the long, high tube of light is performing a specific function on my body. Maybe, as the doctors say, we just have to wait.

An anesthesiologist puts me to sleep, and a surgeon with two assistants performs an endoscopy to remove the battery. The body's internal moisture has activated the battery's current, which has perforated the esophagus with a deep, dark burn. The lithium hidden in the battery's metal heart has been set free. My vocal cords are damaged, and reflux has caused lesions in my larynx. The doctors repair what they can, take careful notes, prescribe medication. After a second operation, I am intubated. I spend three days in intensive care. The extremely high toxicity has spread to the organs connected to the esophagus, and it is vitally important to lower it. Mom paces from one side of my bed to the other. She can't sit down, can't think. Since the damage to my larynx has been severe and my respiratory problems continue, the doctors decide to perform a tracheotomy.

I wake up six hours later and my hands go straight for my throat, though in reality the part that itches so bad is a little farther down. I look for it, fumbling around, and find the plastic. An open protrusion that is now a part of my body. We are asked to be patient, we're dismissed. We'll have to schedule things well in advance with the referral in Buenos Aires, once we're back home in El Bolsón.

It's too late. No one says it, but everyone knows. Just when kids my age are starting to play with more complex words, to discover the strength of tone and the luxury of intentional silences, I lose the few words I had learned. I don't cry, I'm not scared; I don't understand the implications, and there are still many things in this world that fill me with wonder and curiosity.

I like to be bathed. I like when my father sits on the little stool Mom assigned him and holds me in the water to teach me to float. I still haven't done it despite our best efforts, but it's something all three of us still believe is possible. So, supported by the palms of his hands, I go on trying to inflate my belly with air. All he has to do is let go of me, and even so, he can't: my father has changed. He avoids my eyes, his frowning gaze focused on the plastic protrusion of the tracheotomy. *I have to keep the water out,* thinks my father in the bathroom, and at the office in the mornings, and at the grocery store on the way home, and in the car when he's pulling up to the house, *I have to keep the water out.* He holds my body floating on his palms and avoids my eyes that say, *Please! Please! Please!* I want him to let go, and he doesn't know how. He has lost a capacity whose circuit is also connected to his embrace. He can't let go of me, but neither can he hold me. I'm the same size I was a week ago, but there is something in his hugs that no longer recognizes me, something that is misaligned. *What's wrong, Dad? What's wrong? What's wrong?* I want to know, and I keep asking, it's my throat that can't execute the sounds. It's as if all the space in the entire house were entering me through that hole. You have to be able to squeeze the air for the silence to sound like something, but I'm so open that sometimes I get confused—am I inside or out? A body, punctured like this—is it still a body? It doesn't matter, really. The problem is not that I can't speak; the problem is that because I don't speak, he won't look at me.

Mom realizes what's happening, or what is no longer happening, between me and my father. But what can she do? From the very beginning, from the moment I let go of the walls and ventured to walk without holding on to anything, I have been running toward my father. I seek out the madness of intense pleasure that starts with him holding me upside down by one foot, all the energy of his hand embracing my ankle; or attacking my ribs with his fingers; or pressing his lips to my chest and growling so loud that the vibration of his vocal cords makes me tremble inside. And in the moments leading up to that intense pleasure, there is the mutual, theatrical game: my father finds me in my mother's arms, or hugging her legs, and he looks at me angrily, offended. And I scream with pleasure and think, *It's starting! It's going to happen!* And he lets go of whatever he has in his hands, drops it all to the floor, then crouches down and opens his arms to me. He has trained me in this desperation to run to him. I've made a note in my body and my mind that says, *If something happens, he will save me. If something happens, he will come to wherever I am and he'll save me.* And I have stored that note between my heart and spine, right there where everything is most compressed.

Mom is hurt by my preference for him, but everything that makes me happy makes my mother happy, too, just as everything that wounds me hardens her. So now that there are no more theatrics, now that my father's arms have short-circuited and can no longer let me go or hold me, Mom tries to talk to him. At night, she sits on the bed and says, "What's going on with you? Where are you?" She asks it stiffly, her hand kneading a crick in her neck. She walks like that in the morning, too, while she makes breakfast. With her fingers on her neck and her elbow pointing to the sky, Mom looks like a doll hanging from her own hand. She will walk that way all summer, by late spring she will have learned to ignore the pain, and in winter she will drop her arms to her sides, her hands loose but available, busy enough so that her resignation never shows.

Six months later I'm nodding off in my car seat. My thirty-one pounds and five ounces are speeding across the desert toward Buenos Aires. My father is driving. He's tired, and the trip is just getting started. Mom gazes out at the sepia photograph of a silent landscape. She feels untroubled in the car. Enclosed and innocuous, any space she has minutely inspected is a threat-free zone.

The third operation is performed at the Italian Hospital in Buenos Aires. Of all the times I will be exposed to the operating room—four in total during my first six years of life—this will be the only instance when they really hold out any hope. They are parents who still lack the information necessary to understand what is happening. They believe that a young body will be able to repair itself over time, and it is this hope alone, nothing else, that keeps them together.

They settle into a hotel room a few blocks from the hospital and take turns resting so someone is always with me. I am still carefree, because I find joy in everything new, and I'm oblivious to the consequences of this shared, escalating disaster. I make noises instead of pronouncing words, I notice every physical detail of any body language, I copy it all with devout precision.

"Understand?" my father asks at times, sitting beside my bed. He doesn't look at me or expect replies. He reads out loud from children's books, the newspaper, magazine articles. Sometimes he falls silent, or asleep. If he looks at me, I laugh. If he talks to me, I laugh. *Love me, love me, love me,* I think. He can't hear me. My father's state of alarm has been activated and it drowns out any other sound. I should be able to say, *What's wrong? Where are you? I'm okay.* Since I can't speak, I contort my body, my face, my expressions. He doesn't know the body language I've perfected, and the noises I make through the tracheotomy unnerve him. He wakes up and his head jolts upright, and it doesn't seem like he's just returned from somewhere, but rather that he can't believe he is still in the same place. I smile, I laugh, but my good humor is for him another torment.

As soon as I'm released, we head back to El Bolsón. It's a trip of 1,055 miles that we're accustomed to, since we cross La

Pampa every summer to visit my maternal grandparents, who live in La Plata. No matter what, we have to fill up at the gas station in General Acha. Because in the 1990s, besides the fact that appliances are almost always plugged into the walls, gas doesn't get you far, the cars guzzle a lot, and that's the last station until Neuquén.

A little while before the General Acha stop, I start to yawn. For my parents, this isn't just any occurrence, it's a magical thing. Because sure, I am capable of falling asleep in the car, and in fact, once I give in, I can sleep for hours, but there's something about the engine's purr that unsettles instead of relaxes me, and I have trouble surrendering. Then Mom does something she loves to do: she reclines her seat and climbs into the back, takes me out of the car seat, and lays me on her lap. My father used to warn, "That's dangerous." He'd say it once, then again, until she buckled me back into my car seat and returned to sit up front. But apparently my father can no longer tell what is dangerous and what isn't. And since no one objects this time, Mom covers us both with my yellow blanket and we stay in the back seat together. I toss and turn, and it seems like I'm going to wake up. My mother feels her own exhaustion like a yoke, so heavy it competes with her protective instinct. I'm still in her arms, but it almost feels like she could let go, sink into sleep, and drop me. But she doesn't, she holds on, hugs me, and somewhere along this endless stretch of Route 152—*Oh, the miracle at last,* my mother thinks—I fall deeply asleep.

By the time we reach the service station, it's dark out and

there's a line of cars waiting for the pumps. It's Friday in the busy season, and amid the noise of car doors opening and closing, people talking and shouting, my parents do what they can to keep me from waking up. Very slowly, Mom moves out from under me, lays me on the seat, and covers me with my yellow blanket: from my feet, which are always cold, to my head, so the highway lights don't shine into my eyes.

She leans forward and whispers, "You want some coffee?"

My father turns around, gazes at the hair falling long and loose over her chest. After that trip she will always wear it short, she'll stop sharing a bed with him and will come to sleep on a mattress on the floor of my room, beside me, and she will pressure him with impossible demands until he has no choice but to accept a separation.

My father is so tired that he's slow to answer.

"Coffee it is, then," whispers Mom, which means that she has already chosen something for herself.

He watches her get out of the car carefully and walk away, until the honk of a horn lets him know it's his turn. He tells himself, *All you have to do is start the car and move it to the pumps.* The physical exhaustion he feels is dark and menacing.

A tall man moves among the pumps, collecting money. Some months later, searching for information, my father will learn from a local newspaper article that the man is forty-six years old, his last name is Morris, and he inherited that YPF station unexpectedly from an uncle he didn't know he had; ever since then, all he has done is move around those pumps. Ultimately, Morris will state in the article, there's a single instinct that determines everything: you sense which area will complete its cycle first and focus there. While he takes care of the pumps during rush hour, at night he leaves the station in his wife's hands and instead handles the lottery tickets. Pumps or colored boxes, doesn't matter, you have to be ready and pay attention. Two things people often get confused, Morris clarifies, but that are not the same thing.

My father thinks Morris is the man on the phone, because the calls start the day after that first time they speak.

"That'll be twenty-seven pesos," Morris says.

He takes the nozzle from the car's tank, hangs it up, and stands staring at my father. My father is the sort of person who gets out of the car to open the gas tank himself, so he is standing a few feet from Morris as he rummages through his pockets for money, but doesn't find any. He senses the man's impatience. The money must be in his pants or coat, or else in his shirt pocket. He checks in on his own tiredness and tells himself, *And all you have to do now is find the money.* Finally, he has to get back in the car. He searches for his wallet in the driver's side door, in the glove compartment, in his bag. He finds it between the front seats, and when he returns to the pump, Morris is waiting for him with arms crossed. He looks to either side as though monitoring the other pumps, and his voice has changed.

"You like for there to be gas, right?"

My father doesn't understand what the question is getting at.

"Well, I like it when you're ready with the money," says Morris, and my father sees he is chewing something that doesn't look like gum. "Why am I always the one who has to wait for you?"

My father is taken aback. Has this happened before? And why would this man remember him? Maybe it happened on the way to Buenos Aires? Or maybe he remembers seeing a boy with a tracheotomy? My father takes a couple of steps forward to hand him the money and turns back to the car without a word.

Mom isn't back yet, so my father parks beside the line of poplar trees and gets out to smoke, and he watches Morris moving quickly between cars. There are employees in charge of the pumps, but as soon as it's someone's turn to pay, Morris approaches them with his brow furrowed and without a word. It's the customers who have to say hello, thanks very much, and goodbye. Morris only takes the money and nods.

My father leans against the car and looks around for Mom. I'm sleeping on the other side of the glass, stretched out with my feet touching the car seat, and he sees me all wrapped up and almost entirely hidden. Though my head is still covered, my mother had carefully pulled aside the blanket around the tracheotomy: nothing must interrupt my breathing. Only my nose peeks out, and that's what my father finds endearing. He gazes intently at me, and after a long time he spells out my name with the same intensity as on the day they chose it: Elías. Eli. El. He thinks that I have his mother's nose, and he remembers how I scrunch it up, so often, all the time, and it tells him

I'm about to start laughing. He thinks about that, and about his runaway exhaustion, and about the enormous effort he has to make not to start crying.

When Mom comes back holding two plastic cups, he decides to go to the bathroom.

"But your coffee will get cold."

My father passes Morris, who is coming out of the café counting money. He goes into the bathroom and tries to take as little time as possible, because that's how my father does everything now: distractedly but without wasting time. He pees and reads a message someone has written in red on the tiles above the urinal: "Please call." He reads the number over and over and over again, and then he stands in front of a sink at the long Formica counter and looks at himself in the mirror. He hears a voice that disconcerts him. *Am I crazy?* he wonders, because it's Mom's voice that echoes through the bathroom and says, "Excuse me, is there any toilet paper?" But it's only his head running too slowly. The voice is really coming from the other side of the mirror, and another woman answers right away, "There's paper, yes, check the table by the door." Now that he knows she isn't waiting for him, my father turns on the tap, puts his hands under the water, and surrenders to its flow. He closes his eyes for a few seconds, rinses his face, stays a little longer with his hands under the faucet. He has to pull his hands away before he can bring himself to snap out of it, open his eyes, turn off the tap, and leave.

My parents wait for each other by the bathroom doors, and perhaps it's the last time they ever wait for each other. Really, it's my father who waits. As he's standing by the door to the women's bathroom, he sees the car shining among the poplars and wonders for a moment if she'd really left me alone in the car. But Mom comes right out, and they walk in silence. My father opens his door, trying not to make any noise that would wake me. But he sees my mother start opening the back door again, instead of the passenger side. He clicks his tongue and whispers, "Leave him be." He wants to prolong the miracle of my sleep. "Come up front."

Mom knows he is right. She hesitates but concedes, and slowly opens the passenger door, sits down, closes it, slowly, then checks on me in the rearview mirror. Is that yellow blanket warm enough? Is it safe to let me sleep like that? What if the fabric is too tight around the tracheotomy? But she would hear me move, she knows every nuance of my breathing, and silence is the best sign, especially at night. When she closes her door, the light turns off and the yellow blanket darkens, momentarily putting distance between me and my mother's worries. My father starts the car, and now we're back on the road. They drink their coffee, listen to the news with the volume down low, and whisper some indignant comments at the broadcasters. And then, after a long, very long time in silence, and for the first time on this trip, my mother finally gives in: she falls asleep. It's a relief for her and it's a great relief for my father. On the highway, when the silence stretches for so long, he regrets being the only one who cannot sleep, but he is grateful at least for that break when he can be alone.

In a few years, some government office in Buenos Aires

Province will order the removal of the immense sculptures that have been installed every sixty miles on either side of the road, seven of them along that straight, interminable stretch: ruined cars atop metal beams, so twisted and mangled they are almost unrecognizable in the flashes of headlights from sporadic traffic. The surnames of the people who drove them are featured at eye level, in white on a blue plate, with the number of fatalities in red and a warning: "Stay awake, stay safe!" But this accident prevention campaign is still in effect in the nineties, and although my father doesn't slow down, he does turn the radio back on to keep himself awake. Every once in a while, he checks on me in the rearview mirror. From that angle, he can't see my nose peeking out of the blanket, but it's enough for him to remember it. He holds the wheel with just one hand, and after a while switches to the other, a gesture he repeats endlessly. Sometimes he sighs, deeply.

Mom wakes up at the intersection with Route 24, almost an hour later. It takes a few seconds for the fogginess of sleep to dissipate, and she asks my father if he's tired. To make conversation, he tells her what the man from the YPF had said to him.

"Weird, right? That he would remember me . . ."

Mom doesn't answer, she's staring in the rearview mirror. Between one millisecond and the next, Mom has stopped breathing. She jumps, lunges toward the back seat. My father tries to comprehend what is happening, but a truck is coming toward him in the opposite lane and he can't take his eyes off the road. He hears her cry out, and from the corner of his eye he sees my yellow blanket fly violently through the air. Mom is trying to say something between choked screams as she struggles for air. Finally she spits it out: "He's not here!"

My father slams on the brakes, pulls onto the shoulder of the road as quickly as possible. A car passes at full speed, its horn blaring.

"He's not here!" screams Mom. "He's not here!"

"What do you mean he's not here?" my father asks, because what she is saying makes no sense, or is impossible to imagine. And now she's hitting him with her fists. He brings the car to a full stop and turns around. I'm not there. I'm no longer there. I have disappeared.

The blanket is there, and there's Mom getting out of the car, but me, where am I? My father gets out, too, and climbs into the back seat. Outside, Mom looks up and down the highway, yanking at fistfuls of her hair as if something immense was inflating inside her head and was about to break it open. But what is all this pain? Does it have to do with the hole in my throat? Is every punctured thing a wound? An excess of energy in the wrong place?

"But you locked the car when you went to the bathroom, right?" my father yells.

Mom doesn't seem to be in any condition to answer. *Who is to blame this time?* my father wonders. Without waiting for her to get back in, he starts the car, makes a U-turn, and somehow now she's in the car with him. Everything that happens now happens like that, chaotic and jumpy, and at the same time with exasperating slowness. They go back to the YPF in a car that seems to be crawling, though the speedometer displays the maximum speed.

It's strange not to be there. I am nothing of what remains: not the back seat, not the yellow blanket, not my empty car seat. Still, there is something of me in everything that has been mine. *Look at me. Look at me. Look at me,* I say to my father. He grips the steering wheel hard, thinking about his hands under the cold water in the bathroom, about my nose that so resembles his mother's, about his own voice asking me, "Did you swallow something?" and about my voice answering, soft as the line of fog over the whole valley of that desert highway, *Nothing. Nothing. Nothing.*

A car goes by in the opposite direction, and the driver is talking on one of those giant black mobile phones that businesspeople are just starting to carry around. Mom takes several more seconds to compute that she could have flagged him down, they could have tried to stop the car and call the YPF, or the police, though the police are even farther away from that YPF than my parents are. And how would they get the gas station's number? Everything seems disproportionately impossible, though she has never been so alert before.

But me—where am I, if not here? The plastic I breathe through is an orifice, not a nose. I've gotten used to things and people having no smell at all. But something has happened, because there's no way to know what things smell like if the air that enters the body doesn't pass through the head, but even so, I can smell. For the first time in many months: the lavender pine of the felt hanging from the rearview mirror, the new rubber of the car seats, Mom's deodorant. If I'm here, if here is where I'm smelling and yet I don't know where my body is, where am I exactly?

"Shit," says Mom, and she starts to cry. "Shit. He could be on the road," and she stares at my father.

He doesn't seem to hear, or to move his hands at all on the wheel. He is too frightened.

"He can't talk," says Mom. "My son. He's alone, and he can't talk."

And me? From where am I looking at them? Whatever has happened to me, it has turned me into something else. It has disarmed and expanded me, enlarged me. It is a pain that is outside my body. I am an open plastic valve, and whatever is happening inside me emerges and touches others.

When they finally see the YPF station, Mom is so overcome that she moans, clutching the door handle. They drive in, the car bouncing over the curb. When they pull up to the café, before the car even stops, she opens the door. My father turns off the engine, gets out, and stares intently around him: the parking lot, the poplar trees and rest area, the nearby highway. People have stopped what they were doing to turn and look at him. Over by the pumps, Morris starts walking toward him, perhaps to chastise him again, but my father doesn't have time for that and he heads inside as well.

There are customers eating at the tables and others browsing the shelves, but he doesn't see Mom. A lady sitting with her children looks at him and points behind the counter, where there's a door marked PRIVATE. He rushes toward it, pushes it open, enters a dark hallway filled with boxes and merchandise. Mom's sobs reach him as though from the depths of a cave, and my father realizes that he could faint, that there is a possibility, an unacceptable possibility, that he won't make it to the other end.

And then Mom yells, "Who found him?" and my father breathes again. "Where was he?" Mom wails, and my father lets go of the wall and he's almost there, he's almost caught up with her. He sees me, I'm in Mom's arms, I'm hugging her, hiding my face in her armpit. The woman receiving Mom's shouts is nodding silently. She is taller and stouter than Mom, and she seems tired, her shoulders hunched forward, as if she already tried to respond several times and has finally given up. My father is there now, he's here, there's the sound of him panting. We're in the living room of a house connected to the back of the gas station. On the floor there's a pile of wooden blocks the woman has been trying to entertain me with.

"Who was with my son all this time?" Mom wants to stop yelling, to start breathing again, but she can't. She holds me so tight it's as if she were losing her balance, and she really thought I'd be capable of holding her up.

My father knows that if he bends down and reaches his arms out toward me, I will let go of Mom and run to him. He knows the pain a thing like that will cause Mom at a moment like this.

I know it, he knows it, she knows it. And yet: after so long without doing it, he bends his knees, crouches closer to the floor. He looks at me, calls to me, pronounces my name. The vibration of his vocal cords makes my spine quiver. I tell myself, *Don't move.* I say, *No, no, no.* I talk to myself so as not to listen to him. *I don't want to, I can't, it's not enough.* But what is wrong with me? Why am I so furious? There is a hole in my throat, a hole in my body that hurts in theirs. If I stick my finger in there, which one of them do I touch? My father or my mother? *I touch my father,* I think, because I have Mom here, on the outside, because I'm pressing my eyelids against her blouse and that means I can still reach her. So, if I stick a finger in the hole that is mine but that hurts in the body of another, if I probe it, if I prod it, what I touch in there—is that my father?

My father extends his arms to me, he has extended them now, despite the price to be paid. I don't let go of my mother. I refuse, my eyelids pressed to her blouse. My father's voice calls to me again, but I'm no longer able, I no longer want to. I think, *No. No because no. No because it's not the same now.* Mom hugs me. Everything that wounds me hardens her, and there is something in my rejection that unites my parents in a single fear. How is this possible? The child has never rejected his father. Something has happened. What happened? When did it happen? Did someone do something to him?

The woman is talking to my father. "I already told the lady here. My husband found the boy and brought him to me."

"But where was he?" my mother asks.

The woman doesn't know, she didn't ask, should she have asked?

"We waited for a while, didn't we, sweetie?" The woman comes closer, leans over, seeks me out, and Mom pulls me away. "And since he has that little problem," says the woman, stretching the skin of her neck where I have the hole, "we couldn't really talk, isn't that right, sweetheart? So we called the police, just in case. And I have to say, they were very nice, weren't they now?"

The woman looks at me as if I really were following her words. Then she turns to my mother.

"They said they'd come by as soon as they finished their rounds, and that'll be a while yet. Would you like a little something to drink?"

Then Morris comes into the room, and my father immediately stands up. Morris is holding a roll of bills and he crosses the living room to the TV stand. He takes down a small lockbox, opens it, and puts the money inside.

"We feeling better?" he asks, his back still turned.

He closes the box and replaces it, and only then does he look at my father.

"See how fast I always give you what you ask for?"

What happens next is something my father will think about over and over for years to come.

"Follow me," Morris says.

My father glances at Mom and then walks away behind the man. They cross the long hallway to the café and come out again by the counter. On the other side, by the first tables, there is a public phone attached to the wall. Morris takes a token from his pocket and dials a number from memory. His big and battered hand holds the plastic receiver against his ear, and Morris waits.

"I'm calling from the YPF," he says, staring at my father.

He says his name into the telephone, and after a brief silence he bursts out laughing, as if someone on the other end had told a joke. He talks distractedly while he studies my father brazenly, examining his face, his clothes, his hands.

"Yeah, who knows," he says into the phone. "You know how people are these days." He nods. "Yes, officer, of course."

He gives a slight raise of his chin to summon my father. Morris smells of gasoline and tobacco; he hands off the phone and takes a few steps back. My father answers some questions, gives my full name and his own, plus his contact information, including the phone number for the house in El Bolsón. When he hangs up, Morris is no longer in the café.

After a stop in Neuquén to sleep a little, and another seven hours driving the next day, we arrive home. And that same night, finally lying in bed on the verge of sleep, my father is startled by the sound of the phone ringing in the living room. He gets up to answer, and for the first time hears that cold, dark silence that will confound him for years to come. And there are still several more nights that follow when he keeps on getting up. Because someone could call from Buenos Aires with the latest urgent report about my case—at the Italian Hospital, the most critical news had always come in the early morning. He picks up the phone, he always picks up. "Hello," he says.

"Hello!" And it takes him a while to resign himself and hang it up again.

Before the bath, my father checks my body meticulously, including under my arms and between my legs, and even makes me open my mouth. It's not the first time he's done this since our return from Buenos Aires. He doesn't know what he's searching for, maybe marks on my skin, a scrape, but there's nothing at all. He holds me by the arms and lowers me into the tub, making sure not a single drop of water enters the tracheotomy. He wets my hair slowly, shampoos me, making sure the lather drips only down the back of my head, and he takes that moment to check my scalp.

"They had some nice wooden blocks, huh? At the YPF . . ."

He says it as though offhandedly, to see what happens. I concentrate on my knees. Mom thinks something happened to me at the service station when they weren't there, that I'm not the same as before, that something is wrong. My father reassures her, saying I'm just more tired than usual, but that's not what he thinks. He holds me by the shoulders, turns me toward him, kneels beside me.

"And how about the woman? Was she nice to you?"

I nod. My father likes to hold me that way, to see that my shoulder blades are still small enough to fit in the palms of his hands.

"And the man? Was the man nice to you too?" I nod again

and stare into the soap suds bubbling up around my knees. "Did something happen?"

We wait a moment.

"Son," says my father. My father says *son.* "Did someone hurt you?"

I'm furious, just like that, all of a sudden. I am a metal spring that has just escaped from a mattress. I look at him because I can't help it. Twisted, coiled. What is he trying to find out?

"No?" says my father. "Nothing?"

Is he answering himself? Is he answering for me? Is it something he is asking, or something he's concluding?

"You would tell me if someone hurt you? Right?"

I am telling him. Doesn't he see it? I've been saying it this whole time. Wasn't it my father's job to read things on people's faces that they didn't know were written there? What is it that he doesn't see? What is it that he doesn't hear?

Then I pull away, I wriggle out of his hands. If he doesn't see me, if he can't hear me, I don't want him to touch me. What good are his hands holding me in the water? He looks at me in surprise. I grab on to the edges of the tub, holding myself up with a strength I didn't know I had, and I realize I have made the decision not to give this weight to anyone, that I'm not willing to let myself be held ever again.

Late at night, when the phone rings again, my father whispers into the receiver through clenched teeth. "Son of a bitch," he says, and, "I'm going to kill you." He thinks about Morris recognizing me on the highway, carrying me to the café, leaving me in the woman's care. But first, thinks my father, between the moment when Morris finds me and the moment he hands me over, what happens?

"See how fast I always give you what you ask for?"

My father remembers the way Morris asked the question, his sharp, confrontational tone. Is that why he never speaks on the phone? Because he thinks my father could recognize his voice?

After a couple more nights, my father starts to disconnect the phone from the wall before going to bed, and to plug it in again the next morning. During the day, when my father isn't there, people call and they always talk. The silent calls are only for him.

After they've gotten the results of the last surgery, which are meted out from various departments of the Buenos Aires hospital, Mom drags an old mattress to my bedside and permanently moves into my room. She says it's safer that way. A week later she takes her clothes, too, and the room that was theirs becomes only my father's.

Now that he is alone, insomnia slaps my father awake every night. He gazes at the ceiling with adrenaline still tingling in his extremities, as if he had just fallen from the top floor of a skyscraper. It vexes him to waste at night the strength he needs for each day. He gets up and wanders around the house. He turns on the kitchen lights, observes the furniture and appliances, then turns them all off again and moves on to the next light switch. There are two more switches in the dining room, one in the living room, another in each bathroom. Sometimes he comes to my room, but Mom knows about that nocturnal dance and she locks the door. So he keeps walking as far as the phone; he leans against the back of the sofa and stays right there until he's tired enough to go back to bed.

One night he imagines Morris in the café, checking his watch beside the public phone, patiently calculating to be sure that when he calls, he will wake the whole family up. My father goes to the phone and plugs the cord into the wall, so convinced it's going to ring that he keeps his hand on the receiver, ready to pick it up at the slightest sound. And the phone does ring. He grabs it fast, and even faster on the following nights. He learns to hear the click that comes before the ring and to pick up the receiver before the bell even trembles. He learns to lift the receiver to his ear slowly, without saying hello, imposing his own silence, gripping the cord tightly as he waits, feeling himself a part of that mute telephone.

He thinks he is learning to listen, for the first time in his life. He thinks that a salesman exposed to such meaninglessness can only develop extraordinary listening skills. During the time when my mother begins looking into moving closer to a specialized institution where I can start school, my father finds that his telephone sessions bring him an unexpected calm. Whatever it is that comes through that receiver begins to seem ever more familiar. He no longer hangs up but waits to be hung up on. Only then does he unplug the cord from the wall again and feel he can go back to bed and fall sleep.

The arrangement they reach, according to Mom, is the best

thing for me, and my father accepts it without a scene: He will stay in the house, and my mother and I will move to La Plata, the city where her parents live. In exchange, my grandparents will cover my medical expenses and tuition for the specialized school. The salesman with hearing superpowers manages to negotiate a promotion that allows him to pay for a trip to Buenos Aires every month, so he can spend two afternoons with me before returning to the house in El Bolsón, where the phone, now that he lives alone, is always plugged in.

Among mute, deaf, and dyslexic children, I make new friends. I integrate, I progress. Per the school's requirement, Mom learns sign language to help me in my lessons. My father's language is limited to essential instructions like "Be still," "I don't understand," "I love you," and "Time for bed." I know that he also understands the sign for "help," though I've never seen him make it. He would like to learn more, but all his energy is focused on making enough money to pay for the flights to Buenos Aires.

Although I don't utter a word, I read and listen with devotion. I'm fascinated by the English and French comic books that my grandfather reads and translates aloud for me. He is a rigid and constant man who sits with me every night at the edge of my bed, his enormous body sinking so deep into the mattress that we guiltlessly accede to the laws of physics, my body leaning against his, and all of his firmness supporting me with upright elegance. He reads a strip, translates it to Spanish, moves on to the next one. I point to everything I don't understand. When I'm ready to move on, I nod.

At school I start to write, and at home, Grandpa and I have

already read almost everything that he had on hand. So he buys me more complicated collections, and notebooks where we write down impressions of our readings, in French and English. His new hobby is training me in these languages. I absorb everything he offers me, but he doesn't learn a single word of my sign language. After each reading session, he closes the book and I grab one of his hands with both of mine, I jump on him, attack him suddenly while he's distracted. He catches me in turn with one swipe of his paw: the beast I had just trapped now counterattacking, victorious. The theatrics are short and precise. Grandpa grabs me by the wrist and lifts me up into the air. I don't feel the power of my father's hands around my ankle, nor do I hang upside down like I used to love to do. I hang right side up, but at least there is something in that suspension that reminds me of him. Sometimes Grandpa holds me for longer than I can bear. I want to shout, "Stop!" so he'll let go of me, but my body is still exposed to the elements: I open my mouth and my mouth doesn't work. I want to clap twice, which is my way of saying *stop,* but I'm hanging from Grandpa by one hand, and although I hit the other against my chest and against his, he only obeys orders that can be heard, orders in English or French. So I wait. I'm hanging in the air, and I wait.

What happens in the next fifteen years doesn't surprise Mom, or Grandpa, or my father. I achieve everything this family expects from a model child: quick adaptation to each new educational phase, outstanding grades in high school, a scholarship in Buenos Aires. I am fascinated by language; the most precise of them all is also the most abstract, the one that contains all others, so I specialize in mathematical physics, and even before I graduate I accept a job offer at an oil company in Rosario.

My father is proud. At some point over the course of these years he's convinced himself that all he needs to do to help me is to stay on the sidelines, and he thinks that time has only confirmed this theory. It hurts him that I'm so far away, but the only thing he knows how to do with his pain is endure it.

The phone still rings at the house in El Bolsón, though more sporadically now. Once a week, once a month, a couple of times a year. And even though phones have broken free from cords and walls, my father still keeps the landline. He sleeps better knowing the phone isn't disconnected. If it rings, he picks it up, and then he finds it easy to get back to sleep.

At the supermarket one day, he discovers that watch batteries now come with a safety covering to keep babies from swallowing them. He stands there staring at the battery shelf until an employee comes over to ask if he needs help, but he is unable to answer or to buy the product. He returns two days later, because now there is something terribly outrageous about that battery and he needs to take it home and study it. He is in the living room, surrounded by those seven light switches that he has stopped turning on and off in the middle of the night, because nothing has been moved from its place since the day my mother and I left the house, and my father has learned to navigate in darkness. Still, for what he is about to do, he has turned on all the lights. He holds the battery in his hand, looks at it, struggles with the plastic of its hermetic packaging. And now he holds it in front of him. It seems so small it could slip through his fingers, and then he would have to search for it again, as he did so many years ago. Maybe to avoid disaster, my father puts the watch battery in his mouth. He closes his lips and the host settles on his tongue for a second, less than a second: the taste of benzoate explodes in his mouth, burns his tongue. The bitterest substance in this world forces my father to spit. He falls to his knees to fumble on the floor—where is the battery? He wants to find it and put it back in his mouth. He wants to finally understand. He searches, searches again. That the protective coating really does work is even more painful than if it didn't.

I meet up with my father a couple of times a year. I let him know when I'm passing through Buenos Aires on the way to La Plata to see my mother and grandparents, and he hops on a plane to come see me. We sit down at a café near the airport, and my father tells me that the house in El Bolsón finally has a buyer.

"Who is it?" I ask in signs.

"Shoot," he says nervously, "I don't understand."

"Doesn't matter," I say, using my hands again, because "Doesn't matter" is a sign that he did end up learning, since I use it so much.

"I'm moving to Buenos Aires," he says. "We won't be so far away."

I smile politely. I know it doesn't mean that we'll see each other any more often, or that our relationship will change at all. I live in a spacious apartment with three stealthy cats. I have a car from last year and a group of friends I play pool with. I'm in love with a girl who loves me. But he almost never asks about any of that. He still thinks that visiting me means coming to Buenos Aires. It never occurs to him that so many good things could be happening to me that sometimes I go weeks without thinking of him.

The day that he hands over the key to the house in El Bolsón, he also disconnects the landline from the wall for the last time. He packs the device in his shoulder bag, which he puts into the car with other things that he considers fragile. A moving company will collect the furniture and boxes a few hours later, but all the valuable things will travel with him. So, after nearly twenty years, my father is again driving the 1,055 miles between El Bolsón and Buenos Aires.

He starts the trip in the afternoon, stops for the night in Neuquén, and sets off again early the next morning. It's eleven thirty when he approaches the YPF station in General Acha. Now that there are plenty of service stations, now that a gallon of gas gets you twice as far and there is no need to stop, he stops all the same. There are only two cars filling up at the pumps. My father parks under the poplars, even more enormous and silvery than he remembers. He walks toward the café, breathes in the cold morning air, and thinks that between the moment he left the house yesterday and his arrival that night in Buenos Aires, he will live without really belonging anywhere. He exhales conscientiously, realizing what a relief that temporary disappearance is. He hooks his thumbs in his pockets in a new way, a mannerism he has so often seen in men who seem calm and confident. *It's like this, it was so easy,* he almost hears his voice in his head, which is how his own mother had taught him to make wishes.

The old café is now a glassed-in self-service store with automatic sliding doors. Only the long wooden counter, tall and solid, is in the same place, and behind it, with the same PRIVATE sign, is the swinging door he went through so many years ago, looking for me. He is surprised to see that in the corner where the pay phone was, there is now an ATM. Someone says, "Excuse me," and pushes him politely aside. My father is perplexed. He doesn't know what he's come for, and the absence of the phone confuses him. Did he come to talk to Morris? Is it because he sold the house? He came in peace, with no expectations, but now he is wondering what's really happening. Is there going to be a fight, is that it? My father has never hit a man in his life. Is that what he came here to do? "I've sold the house," he'll say to Morris. "Let's see who you fuck with now, calling in the middle of the night."

Although her hair is now lank and white, he recognizes the woman. Tall and stout, she distractedly flips through piles of papers beside two cashiers at the registers. She finds a particular sheet and reads it as she walks away toward the swinging door. Suddenly she stops, turning back to him with her brow furrowed.

"It's you," she says, "the father."

The woman comes around the counter toward him.

"How is the boy?"

She seems moved.

"Good, good, sure. I'm sorry, it's just . . ."

"Does he remember us?"

"Oh, sure." He realizes how nervous he is.

"He gave us such a fright, you know . . . we had no idea where he'd come from, and he couldn't say a word. We didn't know how to help him." The woman sighs and stands gazing at him with her head cocked to one side. "Poor little thing."

She studies my father with nostalgia, as if together they had endured a drama of many days and weeks and now she needed some time to get comfortable in this reunion.

"Come. I want to show you something," she says, inviting him with a wave and walking toward the swinging door.

They walk down the long hallway, still piled high with merchandise. For a moment my father has the feeling that when he reaches the other end he will find me there again, and maybe Mom, too. If it all started over again, would he now have the information he needed to change things? Would he change them if he could? Would he bend down and hold out his arms to me again? Was that what he had done wrong? He wants to understand, but he doesn't understand, and he's frightened to see that the living room is still so much like the one he remembers.

"Look at this beauty." The woman reaches toward a shelf and picks up a picture frame. "I hope you don't mind. It's just that we don't have children of our own, and, I don't know, I like to look at it there with my things."

It's a drawing I had made: a picture of my father, Mom, and me in between them.

"I tried to entertain him every way I knew how," says the woman. "I brought him some wooden blocks we had in the café, I offered him candy, I even let him watch TV with me. In the end, sitting down to draw was the only thing he seemed to like."

In the drawing I have large yellow hands with outstretched fingers, and, at my larynx, a sort of black pendant, big and deformed like a giant eye.

"Oh, but that boy was just so cute, you have to understand that I was captivated. I was already thinking about how to convince Morris to adopt him if no one came for him." She laughs in embarrassment, aware of her own exaggeration.

"But something happened, right?"

"What kind of something?"

My father looks at her gravely. Her smile disappears.

"What do you mean?"

My father feels the anger come on suddenly. It's a pain that straightens him up and disturbs him to the point that he wishes Morris would come in right then and there—it's the perfect moment, now that his body seems ready for an unexpected battle.

"I know something happened." My father hears the change in his own voice.

The woman takes a step back.

"He was a good kid," my father says, "went through four operations and never stopped smiling. But then we left him here with you for half an hour, and he was never the same again."

"But what are you saying?"

Then, yes, Morris comes in. Older, skinnier. He is carrying an open wallet and has a credit card reader at his waist. He crosses the living room in the same direction as twenty years before, probably headed for the same lockbox. When he sees my father, he stops.

"You," he says, lowering the hand with his wallet. "What did you lose now?"

"Morris . . . ," says the woman.

"Something happened to my son," says my father.

"And apparently around here we're always at your beck and call, right?" says Morris. "You already lost him once, remember? You lost him and we found him for you."

"Who found him?"

"I did," says Morris.

"Where was he?"

"By the phone."

"I don't understand."

Morris shakes his head and almost seems to smile to himself.

"Follow me." Morris heads off down the hallway with the same words as last time. My father follows. As he walks behind Morris's tall back, his eyes grow foggy for a second and he makes an effort not to stumble over the boxes. What do they hold? What are those boxes doing there, piled up in the same place for twenty years? The dizziness tingles in his stomach, but he forces himself to keep following Morris, Morris's back like a teetering wall he wants only to crash into. Behind them, the woman's footsteps hurry to catch up. They go through the swinging door. In the convenience store, everything is still in motion.

"Here," says Morris, stopping in front of the small ATM machine.

"This is where the phone was," the woman explains.

Morris picks up an imaginary receiver at the height of his chest and lowers it to a point between his hip and knee. He holds it vertically.

"About this height," he says, and uses the palm of his other hand to mark how tall I was at that age. "Somehow your son managed to get the receiver down, but he couldn't reach the buttons to dial."

Without moving the imaginary receiver, Morris spits something into his hand and puts it in a pocket.

"So I said to the kid, you tell me the number and I'll dial."

The woman nods, confirming the story.

"My son doesn't talk," says my father. He feels so much pressure in his chest that he can hardly use his diaphragm.

"What does that have to do with it? If the kid wants to talk to his father, I dial the father's number."

The pressure is so painful that my father can no longer think.

"But how did you know he wanted to talk to me?"

"What can I tell you? The kid showed me the receiver and I asked, 'You want to talk to Mommy?' And the kid shook his head. Then I asked, 'You want to talk to Daddy?' And he nodded. Is everything this complicated for you?" Morris stares at my father. "I pretended to dial and I let him do his thing. You would have done the same, right?"

My father is crying. Morris widens his eyes, exasperated, disconcerted.

"You know what, I don't follow you," he says. "I don't know what else I can do for you."

"It's just that my son doesn't talk." My father tries to calm down, but it's impossible. "If my son calls me, how will he tell me it's him?"

My father's hands fall defeated to his sides and there's an almost imperceptible movement in his fingers, like those of someone asleep, or maybe dreaming, someone who wants to catch himself as he's falling, or catch something that's in the air and shouldn't fall, and what happens next that morning is no longer important.

Seventeen years later, my father dies, and I have to wait for the doctor to come and write the report. I sit beside his bed in that Buenos Aires apartment that he's never gotten used to, and I tell him, in silence: *Don't worry, Dad, we were happy, at first, and that's enough. Everything's going to be okay, Dad.* And since he doesn't answer, since he has never answered me, I put my finger inside that hole that's like an eye, and I touch inside. I touch my father inside, and I let him go.

THE WOMAN FROM ATLÁNTIDA

She came in to the salon every two weeks. One of us would head her off and lead her discreetly to the back of the shop so the other customers didn't have to see or smell her. They'd sit her down in front of the mirror past the sinks on a bench that we only used for her, and there she would stay, unmoving, until I finished with my customers and turned to her.

Pitys had gotten so old that, beneath her clothes, her shoulders and curved shoulder blades were like those of a little girl in a time-out as she sat wordlessly and waited for me. She wouldn't let me cut or brush her hair, but she allowed me to drape the waterproof cape around her shoulders and wash it. I'd wheel over the portable sink, help Pitys lean back and settle her head under the faucet, and then I'd turn on the warm water and wet her hair, using the back of my hand to keep it from running into her face. After a while she relaxed and closed her eyes. She didn't want me to use combs or brushes, so I applied conditioner even before the shampoo, and that way I could use my own hands to open up the dreadlocks a little so the soap could work into a lather. I stuck my fingers into that long snarl of tangled white hair, and the two of us surrendered in silence to that biweekly cleanse. As soon as Pitys left we would open the front door and the two small windows in back, and we lit the little burner with jasmine oil. The rancid smell of alcohol didn't reach the main salon, but if you crossed the sink area to get to the bathroom or to smoke on the patio, you could tell she'd been there.

I wondered if she had recognized me, if she knew who I was and if that's why she came. Every once in a while I caught her looking at me, and I'd wait to see if one of us would venture to break the silence. I'd first met her almost forty years ago, during a three-week summer vacation. I was ten years old, and my sister was thirteen. I didn't see her again after that trip, and no one ever knew that Pitys was with us when the thing with my sister happened.

And then one day, a whole lifetime later, Pitys stopped in front of the window of this salon and stood staring inside until I went out to get her. When I asked what we could do for her, she opened her mouth, but not a word came out. She studied my face for a few seconds, and finally looked down at her fingernails. It seemed as if she had discovered something new and soul-stirring in them, and I thought about the ceiling fan in her room, about the photograph that she carried in the pocket of her robe, and about the man who had first told us about her. It had been a long time, but could it really be that Pitys didn't recognize me?

—

All that vacation, my sister and I had been sneaking out at midnight, after making sure our parents had finally turned off the lights and we hadn't heard a peep for a good while. We crossed hedges, climbed walls, and slipped into other people's yards. In the warm silence of that big town by the sea, the world seemed open and benign. We went barefoot, since there was sand even in the streets and yards, so soft and white that taking a step in Atlántida felt like a very different thing from a step in the city. But paradise had its limits. Family days at the beach were obligatory and endless, impossible to sabotage. We went down to the beach with everything we needed so as not to leave it again for hours. Our parents' main recreation was for us a daily tedium: we had to forget about the rented house only two blocks away, and act like beings who'd been born and raised right there on those dunes. A simple life in which you could carry everything you needed inside a couple of wicker baskets. A cooler of snacks and drinks, sunscreen, towels, Burako, magazines, radio, mate and thermos, cookies. Dad and Mom lying on one tarp, my sister and I on the other. For all eternity. From their tarp, Mom and Dad sighed and said things like, "We have to make the most of this," and "It's costing us a fortune."

At night, however, while the rest of the neighborhood slept, my sister and I would catch the breath we needed. We'd leave the house with nothing, open to whatever might happen, and the man was always there, even at two or three in the morning, right under the only light in his yard, lying on a lounge chair with his ankles crossed and a Dashiell Hammett book held close to his face. He always wore the same yellow shorts, and only his tank top changed. Sometimes we stopped awhile and tried to make small talk, but he didn't seem interested. I don't remember what we said to him, or whether he ever supplied any comment of his own, I only remember the night he suddenly lowered the book and looked at us in surprise, as if realizing for the first time that we were there.

"And you two?" he asked. "What do you do to keep from getting bored?"

My sister said, "We sneak into other people's houses."

I knew it was a lie, that we only went as far as their patios and gardens, but my sister's exaggeration was always a preview of what was to come, and I nodded devotedly along with whatever it was she was already planning. Then the man asked if we had inspected the poet's house yet.

"There's a poet?" I asked, because until then I'd never heard of a poet who wasn't dead—so she just lived among the rest of the people, just like that?

The man said yes, there was indeed a poet, and it would be good if someone went to see what she was up to. A few weeks ago she'd tried to hang herself from a fan, and in fact it wasn't the first time she'd tried it.

From our hiding spot behind some dwarf pine trees, we saw a house with a line of green tiles below the roof, which the man had told us would distinguish the poet's house from the rest. We circled the building, crouching low under the windows. They were open, with blinds raised and curtains drawn. We tried to peek into one, but it was like peering into a black, empty square. You had to stand there for a moment, very still, and get used to that even darker darkness, before you could finally see anything. I remember the double bed, so close to the window that we could have reached out a hand and touched it. But the sheets tangled up in clothes and pillows made it hard to tell whether there was anyone in the bed or not.

I was afraid of finding the poet hanging from the fan. I didn't know what someone in that state would look like. My sister clicked her tongue at me and ran off, and a second later she was standing on the porch and opening the screen door. We were wearing the denim overalls that were everywhere that summer, which we'd put on over our pajamas before leaving the house. There's a photo of us at the Flamingo ice cream parlor wearing them, my yellow overalls and a one-piece bathing suit underneath, my sister with the fuchsia knot of her first bikini peeking out at the nape of her neck from under her messy curls. Side by side, melting ice cream dripping down our fingers. I have the photo at home hanging on the water heater in the kitchen: one magnet over the blue sky that's now faded to white, another over a blurry, shiny spot that is Dad's finger near the lens. There are no more photos of us together after that. I never again saw my father with the family camera hung around his neck. Sometimes I stand there and study it, and in the image my past self still gazes at my sister in a way that reminds me there was a time when my entire happiness depended on her eyes and on her mood, a time when I would have followed her anywhere as long as, every once in a while, she would click her tongue at me, or, miraculously, call me by my name.

My sister went right into the house. The door leading to the kitchen was unlocked and she just walked in, and I was more scared to stay outside than to follow. We sidestepped empty bottles scattered on the floor, garbage bags, an upended chair, sheets and towels piled by the washing machine. The table and shelves were littered with dirty dishes. The doorway leading to the living room was a large, open archway with withered hanging plants, and we went through it quickly, intimidated by that new, even darker space yawning before us. We crawled in to hide under a side table, huddled together and sheltered by a tablecloth, and from there we stared out at the spectacle of that battlefield.

Moonlight filtered in from the garden and outlined all the things: more dirty dishes, more empty bottles, piles of books, clothes on the floor and draped over sofas, open bags of potato chips. I'd never seen anything like it, and I remember watching my sister's face for some clue as to what was happening, what that place was, what we were doing there. I was afraid that any noise would set me screaming. I tried not to think about the fan, but the image of a pair of feet hanging close to the floor haunted me. In a single movement, my sister sprang out from under the table and I tried to hold on to her, but, as always, she was too far away. She crossed the living room and peered down the hall. I tiptoed over to her, stepping over things on the floor, telling myself, *Don't scream, don't make a sound,* until I was behind her once again with my fingers clutching her shirt and my face against her back. Then we saw the cat, and it's a detail that has stuck with me. In the hallway's depths, the darkness was like a black mouth where you couldn't see a thing, and then suddenly, at floor level, two yellow eyes appeared and stared at us. They didn't blink, didn't even move when my sister took another step toward them. They were so still they seemed like a strange decoration lit up from inside. We stayed like that until finally the cat turned its head. We jumped, and he pushed a door open and went into a room. My sister followed him, my hand again losing the strap of her overalls, and with a few more steps she was inside.

I stood in the doorway and felt the strangeness of occupying that room, the same one we'd seen from outside, through the window. The woman was face down, spread-eagle on the mattress as if she had fallen from above. We stood there, taking her in. It was impossible to tell if she was alive or dead. Overhead, the fan spun slowly, as if about to stop.

Holding on to the bar at the foot of the bed, we waited a little longer until our eyes had adjusted. Then my sister leaned forward and said: "Ma'am . . ."

She reached out a hand to the end of the sheet and pulled it down.

"Hello . . ."

I heard her voice cutting through that absolute silence, and I thought my sister was the bravest person on the face of this earth.

"We want to know if you're okay."

She tugged on the sheet again and uncovered the woman's waist, but there was still no reaction. It was a large bed in a small room, hardly any space to either side—nowhere to move the bed if she were to hang herself from the fan.

Then my sister clapped. It was the kind of thing she did,

even in moments like that. She gave a clap that sounded like an explosion and I had to bite my tongue to keep from screaming. The woman started awake, as if all the sounds had reached her at once. She sat up in bed, disoriented, her eyes open wide. Awkwardly, she settled back against the headboard and rubbed her hands over her face. It was a relief to see she was capable of moving. I wondered if it was possible she didn't see us, because we were standing right there, and yet her eyes never landed on us. She let out air with a long, sad moan, and the cat climbed up and lay across her lap. She had very fine hands with long fingers that extended and contracted on the animal's back, caressing him mechanically. And then it seemed that yes, she finally perceived something, or at least turned her head in our direction. Her fingers stopped and the three of us stayed very still, the cat seeming to wait as well, until he got bored and started licking his paws.

"Do you see me?" she finally asked.

We nodded.

"And you?" my sister asked. "Do you see us?"

"Yes."

The cat stopped its bath and sat motionless, waiting again.

"Well, wonders never cease," the woman said.

She asked if we were from the city council, dragging out her words as if she were drunk, and when we said no she asked if her husband had sent us. It seemed like she was about to get up, so I started to push my sister out of the room, but in the end she pulled the sheet back over her head and we stayed where we were.

"Is it true that you hung yourself from the fan?" my sister asked.

Although the sheet didn't move, we heard a timid "yes," and then a "twice." My sister asked why it hadn't worked the second time, either. I guess she wanted to know whether the woman had figured out what it was she'd been doing wrong, and I thought that if she had learned that, she wouldn't be in bed talking to us. Maybe not fully learning your lessons is ultimately what keeps you alive.

Perhaps because she was a poet, the woman didn't give definitive answers. She replied with phrases like "No one learns from fear" or "If it weighs on you, it's sadness." My sister asked if it was about a man.

"It's never about a man," she said, "even if you think it is."

Her feet were uncovered, and so close to the bar we were holding on to that for a second I imagined myself tickling her; I desperately hoped my sister did not have the same idea.

"It's tedium," the poet said. I thought of the beach and was surprised to find I had a sense of what she meant. Was that what poetry was? A leap to another place without moving at all? "Over a third of a century of tedium . . ." She pointed her toes as if she'd taken a slow leap off a cliff, or as if she felt a sudden cramp. ". . . tedium, and a lack of inspiration."

That word got plastered up somewhere inside my head, a large and shiny sticker with the word "Inspiration." So if people were lacking "inspiration," they hung themselves from the fan? Was "inspiration" what we were searching for at night when we snuck out of the house, or was it something more dangerous that I still didn't understand?

"Is it because you're a poet?"

I was shocked to hear myself speak, to feel the urge to open my mouth and be unable to stop myself. The woman threw off the sheets; the cat jumped down and ran away. After a few seconds, she swung her legs off the bed and finally sat up.

"Who told you that?"

The woman's eyes were on me. A purplish bruise ran across her forehead and part of her nose. She got up, seemed about to fall over again onto the bed, and then recovered her balance. She came toward me as if she were going to lunge at me or strangle me, but she went right past me to the door.

We followed her. She stumbled over things on the floor and grunted, leaning against the wall for support. She went into the bathroom and we were right behind her. She had to hold on to the counter to keep from falling.

"So, you two, are you really here?"

I was distressed that my sister didn't reply.

"Are you ghosts?" When we didn't answer she turned on the light, and all three of us shielded our eyes.

"Vampires, then?" she asked.

I shook my head, taken aback, late to realize it was a joke. My sister frowned, which is what she did when she had an idea, and said: "We are inspiration."

The woman turned on the faucet and stared at us in the mirror.

"Inspiration," she repeated.

"We're here to do our job," said my sister.

The woman bit her lip, as though mulling over the idea. We were so close I could smell the stench of alcohol and days without bathing, and now that I could see her better I realized that, though she was in a bad state, she was maybe around the same age as Mom. She turned on the water and started to wash her face. Then she tried to tie back her hair, but failed several times and finally gave up.

I asked if she was drunk and she said absolutely not, shrinking away as if I were the one who smelled bad. She tried to walk around us and leave the bathroom, but she stumbled and plopped down to sit on the toilet lid.

My sister turned on the bathtub faucet, plugged the drain, and squeezed out a lot of shampoo, which quickly turned into foam.

"And what kind of inspiration would you two be, now?" the woman asked.

My sister told her we were the good kind. Then, with an authority in her eyes that surprised me, she pointed to the tub and told the woman she had added some bath salts, and not to fall asleep in there. She took my hand to leave, and we closed the door behind us, went back to the living room, and turned on the light.

"We're going to clean up this mess," I heard her say.

My sister liked to make what she called radical decisions; she considered it a good exercise and thought it was how you turned things around. I always wondered why you had to turn things around, and what it was that made these decisions radical.

She went to the kitchen and came back with a roll of garbage bags. We focused on the living room and went from top to bottom, collecting things from counters, bookshelves, the table, chairs, and floor. Soon I understood how it made sense to clean a place in this condition—much more sense than cleaning our room at home. There was so much to do here. We put the garbage into one bag, and when we didn't know where a thing belonged, we put it into a second bag. A third bag was for ugly or irrelevant things, because we didn't want the living room to simply be cleaner, what we wanted was to *simplify,* to make space that something new could occupy. "We are invoking inspiration," my sister said several times in a loud voice, as if wanting to be heard from the bathroom. "We are invoking inspiration," I repeated even louder. If the woman really was listening, I wanted her to know that I was there, too, working on whatever it was we were working toward. But not a word came from behind the bathroom door.

We left the garbage in the kitchen, piled atop other full bags, and we took the things we'd decided to eliminate outside, so that none of it would ever enter that house again. We were about to start on the next room when we heard a loud crash in the bathroom, and then another one, metallic this time. The cat scurried in from the hallway, and we ran to see what was happening, opening the bathroom door without knocking. The woman was on the floor beside the tub, wrapped in the shower curtains that she had pulled from the rod, which had been yanked down and broken. She hadn't even taken off her clothes, and the water was about to spill over. We went to her and helped her up. My sister turned off the tap.

"It's my head," said the woman.

I wondered if she was talking about inspiration again, but then she touched the back of her skull. There was blood on her fingers, and she stared at it in fear. I thought about calling Mom and Dad, or an ambulance, but I was afraid of admitting to what we'd been doing all those nights. So I suggested we get the man in the lounge chair.

"No! Please, not my husband."

Maybe the blow had cleared her head. That man was her husband?

"Please, no."

She glanced toward the hallway.

"There's antibiotic cream in the other bathroom, and gauze. We have everything we need."

My sister looked at me and jutted her chin toward the door, and I went to get the supplies. I walked down the same hall that had scared me so much just a couple of hours earlier, and I felt strong and in charge. My big sister and a woman who was also a poet who'd tried to kill herself over a lack of inspiration both thought that I was capable of going to a totally unfamiliar bathroom, finding gauze and ointment without instructions, and returning just like that. It was a triumphant feeling that uplifted me, and the revelation that I was up to the challenge made things happen in turn: The bathroom was at the end of the hall, the gauze in the third drawer, a blue plastic jar at the back of the medicine cabinet said "antibiotic" in red. I thought about school, about how and to whom I would tell the story of what was happening. But when I went back to the first bathroom I found the woman already on her feet, her head under the sink faucet, my sister helping her get cleaned up, and I felt like I'd somehow been cheated. My sister's fingers were in the woman's hair, helping to wash away the blood while keeping the water out of her face. Both of them were silent, and yet I had the feeling I'd interrupted something. I wondered what kinds of things a poet might do or say when you were left alone with her. Would my sister tell me later if I asked?

We sat the woman back on the toilet lid and took turns pressing a wad of toilet paper against the wound. We waited that way until the blood lessened and we could use the antibiotic cream. I dried her hair slowly with a towel, lock by lock. I liked to touch her hair and she let me do it, staying silent as the towel turned a damp pink. I wanted her to smell better, and I was willing to bathe her, brush her hair, open her drawers until I found something that looked good on her.

At the salon, every time Pitys lay back at the third washing station and closed her eyes, I massaged her scalp and concentrated on her body's fragility, and on my uncanny desire to take care of her; that is, I copied the movements I'd seen my sister make that night, so long ago. At an age when I didn't know that a younger person even could protect an older one, my sister had taught me to move the woman's head from side to side using only one hand, with no need to put down the sprayer. In addition to the sand that washed away with the rest of the dirt, I would often find little shells or pebbles among the tangles of hair. Several times I asked around to see if anyone had ever seen her at the beach, but even in a town as small as Atlántida there were people who had never seen her at all, not at the supermarket or the pharmacy or anywhere else, people who didn't know who this poet was or where she lived. How was that possible, after so many years? And where did the shells come from, if she never went down to the beach? Did she swim in the ocean at night, when the shore was completely deserted?

Every time she came in, I got her hair smelling like chamomile again. When I took off the cape she would gaze at herself in the mirror, narrowing her eyes a little as if some glare I couldn't see were blurring her vision. She left the salon the same way she entered: dignified, without asking questions or permission, without paying for the wash or leaving a tip. And two weeks later, when she came to stand in front of the window again until we brought her inside and settled her in the back, her whole being smelled again of sea, of alcohol and dead sea snails.

That summer, we went back to the poet's house every night. The first time, we just wanted to make sure she was still alive, that the blow to the head hadn't been serious and she hadn't bled out in that living room we'd left so impeccable. During the day, at the beach, we had placed our bets. Would she be alive or dead? Would she be writing? Hanging from the fan or sprawled in the bathroom again? Did she ever leave the house? In what condition? And if she finally had managed to kill herself, would we take the cat or abandon him to his fate? Would we tell the police or leave everything as it was? We'd have to at least let the man know, especially if he was her husband.

In order to talk out of earshot of Mom and Dad, we got in the water and floated between the waves. When the crests grew too high, we had to duck all the way under the water and let the wave pass overhead, or else we'd end up curled into a ball on the shore with tons of sand in our hair and swimsuit. There's a reason they call this beach the rough one. But I liked those violent interruptions from the sea, they gave you time to think even as they took it all away in a second. "Incoming!" we'd shout, ducking under as fast as we could to meet the current holding our breaths, until we felt the crest of the wave push us violently backward.

"What if we get there and she's gone?" my sister asked when we came up for air.

"Incoming!" I shouted again.

I went under and felt grateful for the water's cold silence. I could accept any outcome for our wagers, except returning and finding that the woman wasn't there. She was something we had discovered all by ourselves, a treasure that belonged to us. Alive or dead, the woman was ours, and if we left her at her house in the morning, that's where we wanted to find her at night when we went back. Our meeting with the poet seemed like an unheard-of privilege, no matter how damaged she was. She was a secret we wanted to shout nonstop, but we only shouted between the Atlántida waves, out where no one could hear us. There, floating close together, we promised each other that no matter what happened, we would never tell anyone about the poet we had stashed away.

We finally made it through all those daylight hours that had to be endured before night could come. Finally, the lights in our house were turned out, finally the silence, the getting out of bed on tiptoe, the slipping out without a sound, climbing a wall, opening the gates, petting the Labrador in the yard with lemon trees so he would whine quietly instead of barking at us, going the long way around the block to avoid the man who still read every night in his yard, sliding sideways through the shrubs to reach the poet's house.

That second night we found her going through the garbage we had piled up in the kitchen. She didn't want to tell us what she was looking for, but every once in a while she returned to the bags and started rifling through them again.

"Everything's a mess!" she complained in one of her comings and goings, glancing around at the neat living room.

She had more energy than the day before, but she was also drunker. My sister told her that if she wanted inspiration, then we were going to have to do a few exercises. She pushed aside the coffee table in front of the sofa and told the two of us to lie down belly-up and close to each other, because we were going to do a meditation that would induce introspection. Where had she gotten an exercise like that? Was it something she had learned, or was she making it up? I asked why I had to do it too, and my sister explained that if inspiration wasn't taking hold of the poet's body, then it would have to enter mine, and from there my sister would take care of moving it into the poet's. That seemed reasonable to me, and we lay down on the floor. Her relaxation instructions were so good that I struggled not to fall asleep, and that time, and almost all the following nights when we repeated the inductive meditation, I woke up to my sister yelling, "Hold hands! Hold hands!" because that was how I had to pass on the inspiration. But even though the woman squeezed my fingers hard every night, nothing ever moved from my body into hers.

In addition to the inspirational exercises, we cleaned both bathrooms. En route from one to the other I saw on the wall, among decorations, mirrors, and postcards, a photograph in which I recognized the woman. She was sitting in a bar with a dozen or so other people. Except for one other woman next to her, they were all men. Were they also poets? Where were all those people now? Did they know the woman was out of inspiration?

We threw away practically everything, except for a couple of towels in good condition, an unopened bottle of perfume, and a little box that held rings and bracelets. We brought toilet paper from our house because the poet was out and we had our needs, too, and also a spiral notebook of my sister's that she wasn't using. It was graph paper the size of an open palm, which we thought would be ideal for poetry. Since the woman seemed prone to losing anything at any time, we attached a pen to the spiral with a string. Then we looked around for a thicker and more elastic band, one that wouldn't hurt her skin, and in the end we took the ribbon belt from one of her dresses, cut it in half, and used it to tie the notebook to her wrist.

"Always remain connected to your material," my sister said.

She adjusted the knot on the notebook and the one on the woman's wrist several times to make sure everything was well attached. We knelt down in front of her and kissed her hand.

"You are blessed," I said.

I didn't have my sister's eloquence or rigor, but I was starting to sense that if you wanted something to have an effect on the poet, it was good to close the phrases that my sister opened.

"What are your names?" the woman asked us.

My sister didn't answer, so although I was dying to say my name, I kept quiet too.

We figured that during the day she slept, wasted time, and drank the several bottles of wine that we later collected and took out with the trash. But what else did she do? If she didn't clean, or cook, and had no one in her care, how did she spend her hours? What did it mean to do poet things, and how much time did they take? And the alcohol—was that required? We knew how the empty bottles left the house, but where did she get the full ones? She didn't seem in any condition to go out, so she must have the bottles hidden away somewhere, though we still hadn't figured out where.

We started every session by finding the woman in the house and convincing her to let us lead her to the toilet, where we sat her down for an initial cleaning. We put soap on a wet towel and wiped her face and armpits. It was so hot that she was almost always wearing tank tops or sleeveless shirts, but one time she had on long sleeves and we tried to undress her for the cleaning. She leapt to her feet, startled, and wrapped her arms around herself, then locked herself in her room for a good while. One time we waxed her mustache, and if you held up the wax strip to the light, the hairs were a lot thicker than they looked on the skin. Sometimes we swabbed her ears, or had her swish mouthwash and spit. She wasn't always sober enough for that, though, and then we would just have to endure her disgusting bad breath the whole night.

We'd check the notebook to see if she had written anything. She almost never had, or else what she wrote seemed to us like anything but poetry. She made a shopping list once, and another time she'd jotted down a phone number. Whose number? She couldn't remember, or didn't want to tell us. The prospect of opening the notebook and finally finding a poem thrilled me. I wondered what subject she would choose and how it would arise. Was it something she had to come up with herself, or did she have to find it somewhere? And if she found it, how did she know that it was what she was looking for?

"Do you think she'll still have the notebook attached tonight?" we wondered aloud between one wave and the next. In a fit of clarity, the poet had lengthened the ribbon on her own by adding a string, and now it was long enough that she could put the notebook into her back pants pocket. It was a miracle she hadn't cut the string, or that the notebook hadn't ended up soaked in pee or covered in tomato sauce from those half-finished plates of pasta we found all over the house.

There were bookcases to either side of the fireplace. My sister assured us it was an important exercise to take down the books one by one, read each title out loud, and return it with the spine facing in. "With titles hidden," my sister intoned, "the poet's thirst will ignite." I climbed up onto the ladder and handed the books down to them. For a while the poet followed the rules and read the titles as we passed them to her, but sooner or later she'd get up from her chair and start to wander around. Once she lost interest, she only wanted to escape. She'd lock herself in the bathroom to cry, or she'd climb into bed, or disappear into the utility room, which had one of those old-fashioned locks that can be turned from inside.

"Do you know my name?" she asked us once.

"It's best not to name things," said my sister.

I was sorry for her bluntness, but the woman looked thoughtful. She was clutching the notebook so tightly it seemed she could open it at any moment. I wanted to finally see her write something down, and I sat wordlessly waiting. But no miracle happened then, either.

When we were in the ocean, between one wave and the next, we called her "our poet." My sister said that if we knew her name and there were books by her in the house, then we would be tempted to read and judge her, and if we really were inspiration, we had better act without prejudice. I thought of all those shelves with the book spines turned inward. Had we made her read the titles of her own books?

"But it's cruel not to ask her name."

"Incoming!" my sister shouted, and before ducking underwater, she smiled mischievously.

If we saw other women her age at the beach, it was startling to see them so fresh, laughing and chatting so lightly. We watched them talk or nimbly rub sunscreen on one another, and they seemed like animals of a different species, maybe more like our mother's, but definitely the opposite of our poet's. We liked ours the way she was, so weird and so gruff. And yet, sometimes when we got to her house she would already be sitting on the toilet, ready for her initial cleaning. We'd brush her hair back and tie it into a long, straight ponytail. One time we tried putting makeup on her, but she looked weird that way, so we washed it off and left her how she was.

We organized the kitchen, checking the backs of every single cabinet. It seemed obvious that it was there, in some secret corner of this room, where the woman must keep the bottles of wine. It took us two nights to examine, purge, and reorganize everything, and we still couldn't find her stash.

"Do you think she can leave the house?" I asked my sister once while we were in the water. "Do you think she buys her own food?"

We ducked under to let a wave pass and came back up for air.

In spite of the half-finished plates of pasta that sometimes appeared, we never saw her eat, and she was thin.

"We could cook for her," my sister suggested.

I remember a strong wave, the kind that sends you rolling even if you go underwater to dodge it, and I reemerged facing the shore. That's when I saw the man.

I recognized his tall, long-limbed figure. His back was to me as he talked to Mom while Dad struggled with a sun umbrella a little farther away. It took me a few seconds to react, and then I shook my sister and pointed. It was him, the man who read every night on his lounge chair.

"What do we do? What do we do?"

What was he saying to Mom? My sister was already swimming toward them, and I followed. What if something had happened to our poet?

We swam to the shore, and by the time my head was out of the water again, my father had joined the conversation. The man pointed off somewhere among the dunes, right toward the block where we all lived. He was wearing the same yellow swim trunks we'd seen him in the first nights, flip-flops on his feet and a towel slung over his shoulder. He had set a grocery bag at his feet and was nodding at whatever Mom was saying. As we emerged from the water I glanced at my sister to exchange impressions, but she was running full speed toward the man, as if she planned to put a stop to that meeting by simply crashing into him. A few feet before she reached them she slowed down, turned, and went straight to her towel. I imitated her. I copied the way she coiled her hair to wring out the water, adjusted her swimsuit, and flopped onto our tarp. We stayed there lying face down, frozen and staring into each other's eyes, as if we had just died but still had enough time to overhear a few words before descending into hell.

"How awful," said my mother, who hadn't even turned around when we came over. "Thanks for letting us know."

My father was standing, and he took a step toward the man to shake his hand.

There was silence, and then we heard the man say, "These girls must be your daughters . . ."

I peeked at him for a second out of the corner of my eye, and he was looking at me and nodding.

When the man said goodbye, he leaned over to pick up the grocery bag. And then we saw them, saw and heard them, all those bottles clinking together. Four or five full, shining bells. We had imagined them hidden somewhere in the house, but the man's mischievous glance when he passed us corrected our assumptions. I was waiting for him to get a little farther away before I leapt at Mom to ask what he had said. But my sister didn't take her eyes off me, and she slowly put a finger over her mouth to order silence. She only moved it to whisper: "In the water!"

And although my legs were trembling from the effort of staying afloat all day, I followed her without question.

That night, when we performed our general inspection of the house, not only did we find the usual empty bottles, we also identified the bag we had seen on the beach, now lying on the kitchen floor. The bottom of the plastic had been torn as though the bottles had been removed from below, but the handles were still tied the same strange way we'd seen earlier that day. First a tight knot and then a bow, as if it were a gift.

When we sat the woman down on the toilet to start our ablutions, she was just as drunk as ever. I wet a beach towel and washed her face and armpits. My sister checked to be sure the pen was still tied tightly to the notebook's spiral, and the notebook still well attached to her wrist. Then she opened the notebook, paged all the way through it, and shook her head at me, which meant that once again there'd been no meaningful progress.

"Why don't you talk to me?" asked the woman. "Why don't you ask me things?"

We looked at her in surprise. Accustomed as we were to her silent obedience, it was strange to hear her speak. I thought she was absolutely right. Why *didn't* we ask her things? Did she have kids? Maybe daughters our age? What if they were dead and that was why she liked having us around the house? *Did* she like having us around the house? And the man, was he really her husband? But my sister was watching me, her finger already rising toward her lips. Then she turned back to the woman.

"If you seek inspiration . . . ," she said, nodding at me to finish.

". . . you must surrender to the void," I blurted without thinking.

Maybe the woman couldn't find inspiration because we were there siphoning it off all night. What if our energy as we moved, our eagerness for everything, was actually confusing her even further?

That night, we decided to clean the woman's room. To keep her entertained while we worked, we sat her in a chair in the hallway, and my sister stacked seven books of poetry on the floor to her right. The exercise consisted of picking up each book and reading only the first line out loud before placing it to the other side; when she'd read all seven first lines, she was to start again in the opposite order, reading only the second line, then the third, and so on. We listened to her voice, intoxicated but musical on some lines, distracted at times and at others oddly focused, while we got down to work. We took all the clothes that she surely hadn't worn in years, including coats, long dresses, and all kinds of shawls, and put them into bags. We also took out and bagged purses and shoes that were broken or in poor condition. Belts, brooches, and all kinds of things that were ugly, too wrinkled, cheap, or just not good enough for a woman like ours. We tried on some hats and went over to dance or jump around in front of the poet. Once or twice she looked at us attentively and an idea or a memory seemed to show on her face, but mostly she stayed engrossed in her assigned exercise and didn't even glance up at us.

My sister wrote "Free to take" on each of the seven bags, and I lugged them out to the sidewalk one by one. Since the woman was still reading, we sat down to rest for a while on the sofa. The lack of a TV in that house felt strange, and I entertained myself by checking that nearly all the places where you could set things down had marks left by wineglasses. They had easily come off of the glass and plastic surfaces, but the wood, leather, rugs, and brick floor were all materials we'd failed at cleaning.

The woman's robe lay on the floor, and I took the chance to go through its pockets. I found a passport-sized photo of a girl my sister's age, which we studied for a long time. The girl resembled the poet—could she be her daughter, or her sister? Or maybe the woman herself as a child?

Before we left, my sister announced that we were going to need a large sheet of paper, at least the size of a person's head. There was paper all over that house: in the books, in the woman's used notebooks, in newspapers and magazines. But my sister wanted it blank, and by then I was so tired that I just sat down in the living room while she came and went. I had never in my life seen my sister give up. Suddenly she stopped and turned toward me, illuminated. It took me another second to look back at the woman and understand what was happening, but the poet had anticipated my sister's intentions and was hugging the little notebook to her chest. My sister leapt onto the sofa, jumped over its back like a circus acrobat, and hung around the woman's shoulders while the woman lurched from side to side, trying to shake her off. I stood up from the sofa and took a few steps backward. What were we doing in that house? What were we really doing to that woman? She was our poet—were we going to leave her just like that, from one day to the next, when vacation was over? Would she think about us? Would she miss us? Should we get her phone number and call her every once in a while to see if she would answer? Should we send her postcards? And who would wash her every day? If in our absence she hung herself from the fan again and finally managed to kill herself, would we be responsible?

My sister broke loose. She had managed to wrest the notebook away from the poet, yanking the string from her wrist, and the poet was holding one hand with the other as if to stop it from bleeding. It was like my sister had torn out her heart and carried it a few feet away to see if it would keep on beating. My sister turned the pages and tore out six blank ones. Then she returned the notebook, but roughly, and the woman was left clutching it tightly, unsure what to do, so lost and desolate that I went over to her, took her by the hand, and led her to sit down on the sofa. I retied the string around her wrist, fixed her hair, which had come undone, and said, "Do you want to tell us your name?"

I felt like that would soothe her.

"Yes, please," she said, but instead she started to cry.

I had to sit down next to her and stroke her arm for a while, until she finally grew calm again.

"My sister used to call me 'Pitys,'" she said.

I would have liked to ask where that sister was now and why she'd called the woman that, but I knew my own sister would punish any question I asked.

"I'm an alcoholic," she said.

I laughed. By that point her confession seemed too funny, and I couldn't help it, though I was ashamed.

"I do it out of necessity," she said.

That struck me as logical, so I nodded to show I understood.

"When I'm sober, I'm a danger to others," she said.

I glanced around for my sister, wanting her to hear this, too, now that after so many days of silence, the poet was finally sharing something personal. But where had she gone? I found her in the kitchen sitting in front of the six notebook pages that she'd stuck together with Scotch tape: now she had her blank page the size of a head.

"Pitys," I said, "her name is Pitys!"

A second later I remembered my sister's belief that it could be dangerous to know the woman's name. She shot me a severe look, but a moment later, to my surprise, she nodded and turned back to what she was doing. She had cut out letters from different magazine headlines and was taping them to the paper one by one. She held it up for me when she finished, and it said, "Come in and I'll call the police." We didn't know if the trick would work, but it couldn't hurt to try, at least for one night. We also discussed what could happen to a drunk if she stopped drinking for a day. Would she be in a better mood? A worse mood? What if she was suddenly cured and she locked up the house and wouldn't let us in, either? The important question was whether a day without alcohol would kill her—my sister said that could happen with drugs if you stopped them cold turkey. We decided the risk was worth it and went out to hang the sign on the front door. While my sister held it up, I put lots of Scotch tape around the sign's edges. My sister gazed at me for a moment as though really seeing me, and I looked at her arms, strong and outstretched, velvety from the salt water, and I had a crazy desire to bite her or tell her I loved her. During all of those days, there was never a more perfect moment to have given her a hug. If I hadn't taped the sign so well, if it hadn't held up in the morning dew, would things have been different?

We woke the woman, who had fallen asleep on the sofa, and dragged her back to the toilet. The three of us in the bathroom once again.

"Pitys," my sister said, holding the poet's hands between her own. "Tomorrow will be a total block."

The woman stared at her, startled. She pulled her hands away and held tightly to the edge of the toilet lid.

"It will come," I seconded her, since nothing more interesting occurred to me.

"What?" the woman asked. She was paying close attention.

"It will knock at the door," said my sister. "It will have his voice."

"His voice?" She peered at us fearfully.

"If you answer, inspiration will disappear forever."

My sister reached out to close the bathroom door, and the woman shook her head.

"You have to stay in here."

"All day?"

I was shocked to hear the woman ask so many questions, almost like we were having a conversation.

"The total block will enter through the chimney," said my sister, pointing upward and toward the living room. "It will flow like smoke along the floor, through the whole house, searching out the wettest places."

The skin on the woman's arms had goosebumps, and I felt

her shivers spread to me. In the bathroom, my sister's voice echoed off the tiles with a deep, divine authority.

"It will come to the bathroom, and in front of the bathroom it will stop."

"Why?"

"Because it will see this crack." My sister pointed to the thin space between the wooden floor and the door, a long dark line that seemed sinister to me.

"It will read the light as a threat," I said.

"It will not enter," said my sister. "But if you come out to let the man in, the block will find you."

All three of us shook our heads, which seemed to me like an unequivocal sign of success.

At the beach, we floated between waves almost all day long. There were too many things to think about and discuss. What if the poet let the man in anyway? What if she didn't open up but the man still handed her the bottles through the window, or left them right there at the door?

We had filled the tub with blankets and pillows and left books for her, plus a glass so she could drink all the tap water she wanted. We cooked a whole box of spaghetti with two cans of tomato sauce, ate half of it, and left her the rest with a fork.

What was the woman doing right now? We wondered this in the morning, and then at noon, and later after lunch, and in the evening before leaving the beach, and in our house while our parents made dinner, and in bed while we waited for silence, lying there in our clothes, counting the seconds that numbered into the thousands and seemed never to end.

At the poet's house, the sign was still taped to the front door. It was unlocked, as always, and everything inside was just as we'd left it. We crossed the kitchen, the living room, and the hallway without seeing a single bottle. The bathroom door was still closed. We knocked a couple of times.

"Pitys?" we asked.

We opened the door, and at first, in the darkness, we couldn't see her. A woman takes up a lot of space, she's not an easy thing to lose in a small bathroom, but we had to look closely to find her, curled up in the bathtub among the blankets and pillows, fast asleep. It was a tranquil and tender scene. When we turned on the light she covered her face with her hands, then rubbed her eyes and nestled in serenely. She had eaten all the spaghetti and the water glass was on the edge of the tub. She had been playing with her makeup, which was spread out on the counter under the mirror, though her face and hands were clean. The toilet paper had been unrolled into a big puffy pile between the bidet and the toilet.

The woman slowly sat up and seemed pleased to see us. Her mouth was twisted strangely in an expression we'd never seen her make before, and when she tried to shift positions I realized her hands were trembling a little.

"Look," she said.

Still a little drowsy, she struggled to move among the blankets. Finally she managed to turn around and sit up a little closer to us. My sister perched on the bidet and leaned toward her—what did she want to show us? I sat on the edge of the tub. The woman had untied the notebook from her wrist and she handed it to my sister, open. Had she written something? Her script was shaky, but my sister deciphered the words one by one, reading them aloud:

I get bored,
I get sick,
It's simple, I say.
Everything that happens
From the skin in
Has to be this that I am.

It didn't make much sense to me, or seem all that poetic.

"Is it about your sister or about your husband?" I asked.

"It's beautiful." My sister was moved.

She was gazing intently at the poem, in a way I'd never seen her read before.

"I need to get out," the woman said.

My sister stood up and waited for her at the threshold of the bathroom, holding the notebook so tightly between her open palm and her chest that I wondered if they were going to fight over it again. By that point, did the notebook belong to my sister or to the woman?

"I mean get out of the house," the poet added.

I was alarmed. Going out was dangerous. If we let her move around of her own volition, could we lose her? She turned and leaned back in the bathtub, hung her legs over the side, and pulled herself up with her arms. In one hop she was on her feet. She was the same woman as always, and yet there was something new in her. She looked in the mirror and washed her face, without any need for us to do or say anything. Was it really that easy? Just stop drinking for one day, and inspiration will seep in through a dark crack and wake you up with all this energy? With wet hands she pulled her hair back in a high, messy style that would never have occurred to us and that suited her wonderfully, and she left the bathroom even though my sister hadn't given her a yes or a no. What if outside she took off running and wouldn't stop? How would we catch her? I glanced at my sister, but her eyes held something very different from my fear, something curious and voracious, and a second later we were following the woman around the house. She went to her room, put on a pair of jeans and a T-shirt.

"Who wants chocolate milk?" she asked.

She opened the kitchen cupboards one after another. We had cleaned so much that some of them were totally empty. The little that remained was organized by size and color, and neither of us remembered where the boxes of powders were. In the end she filled three coffee mugs with water, but after the first sip she poured it into the sink and stared at the ceiling.

"Do you think you can write more?" my sister asked.

The woman nodded with such certainty that I started to question what my sister was really asking her.

"Do you think you can teach me?"

The woman nodded again, and said: "Let's go to the beach."

"Not a chance," I said.

But they were already headed outside.

I was uneasy walking around with the two of them, getting farther away from that house and from ours, even from the man's. The night appeared more sinister beyond the block where we lived, and the woman, beside my sister, was smaller, younger, almost weightless.

We crossed another street and descended to the dunes, and then we were too close. What if she wanted to get into the water? We were barefoot, and I was surprised by how cold the sand felt at night. It seemed like a different place from the one our parents dragged us to each morning of our vacation. Then everything happened fast. The woman saw the ocean, peeled off her T-shirt and jeans, and sprinted toward the water in her underwear. My sister still held the notebook, but handed it to me as soon as the woman started running.

"Don't let it get wet!" she ordered.

She started running too, still dressed in her yellow overalls with her pajamas underneath. The two of them seemed the same size, and although I knew it was because the woman was farther away, the resemblance took me aback. I pretended not to know which was which, and I understood how much I loved them both. I pressed the notebook tightly against my body, and I saw them move into the water. They splashed each other and shouted amid the thunder of approaching waves. At some point one of them ducked underwater, then the other, and now they were just two heads coming up for air. Were they swimming out to sea? The crests rose up furiously, the waves were too high. I walked toward the water, then started to run. I knew how far it was to the water's edge, my sister and I raced there every morning, and yet that night I ran and ran and the sea had recoiled so far that I could never catch up. Then the woman's head disappeared. I reached the water and took a few more steps. My feet were so cold they hurt. I was in charge of the notebook, I couldn't get in, but the second head was nowhere to be seen. I saw a wave rise up behind my sister.

"Incoming!" I shouted to her.

I wasn't pretending anymore, it was a huge wave, but I knew she was too far away to hear me. She ducked underwater in time, and the wave grew until it seemed an extraordinary thing, the tallest wave I had ever seen. It crashed along the sand, unfurling rapidly toward me, fizzing as it encircled my legs, climbed up to my hips, and then retreated back into the sea. I didn't see either of the two heads. I had stopped breathing. I squeezed the notebook, warping the spiral against my body. And then, finally, a head appeared. Just one. I screamed, waving my hands and jumping up and down. Two arms appeared on either side of the head, but it was unclear whether they were waving back or doing something else. The head rode the momentum of another wave, but it withdrew again a moment later. The figure lay on its back, as if it needed to rest in order to keep going. When I realized it was the woman's head, I wanted to drop the notebook. I screamed again; really, I hadn't stopped screaming that whole time. I screamed my sister's name with all the air in my lungs, as if I could send it into hers. The woman's head sank under and re-emerged several times, and it seemed that now she was swimming. Every once in a while she stopped and turned toward the open sea. She was shouting, her hands cupped around her mouth, elbows bent to the sides—but what was she shouting? The noise of the waves kept me from hearing. Did she know my sister's name? Now she could touch the bottom and her shoulders came out of the water, her torso turning desperately this way and that like an out-of-control radar. Her body emerged further, her head hoisted atop it and swaying clumsily. She's coming back, I said to myself, she's closer now, she is getting out of the water without my sister. My knees were shaking so much that I finally let myself fall. First to my knees, then also my palms against the sand, the sea smacking me in the face over and over. I breathed, and although water entered my nose and ran down my throat and into my stomach, I breathed again and thought about maybe drowning, and also about the woman's fan, and then I noticed I had let go of the notebook and was scared when I understood that I wasn't going to do anything, I was going to let it go. The water rose and lifted me with it, and when it receded my hands met sand again. I thought that if they touched something now on the ocean floor, it could be my sister. An arm, a foot—I was ready to grab on to whatever I found. And a second later my head was somewhere else, and there was no more need to cling to anything.

The momentum pulled me upward, from my stomach. It wasn't something I was doing, it was the woman picking me up, pulling me out of the water with a strength I never imagined she'd have. I was in the air, my head hanging down and eyes staring blankly at the boiling foam below, my arms and legs dangling loose. A wave knocked us over but she picked me back up. With long strides, she finally got us out of the sea.

She collapsed onto the sand. Part of her body fell onto mine, and that's how we stayed. A lighthouse blinked in the distance, white and tiny, not bright enough to illuminate us, seeming to have only enough strength for itself. It turned on, then off, then on again. It felt like each flash took longer than the one before, as if it wanted to stop. And yet it pulsated for hours, and then for days, and weeks, until at the moment I least expected it, the woman pulled away from me. Her torso sat up first, still soaking wet, white and violet like marble. Then she stood up with a painful sigh. I reached out my hand and touched her cold, bare ankle. She stayed motionless for a second, waiting for the energy of my movement to run out. When my arm fell back onto the sand, she took in a big breath, and without saying a word, she walked away.

At my mother's request, my aunt came to Atlántida to take me back to Buenos Aires. My father returned home a week later, and my mother nearly a month after that. There were no more family vacations. I finished grade school and high school, then attended college for a few years but didn't graduate. Mom and Dad sold the house and moved to a smaller apartment. I got married and had two children who kept me busy until their adolescence. When they started to go out, I remembered how lonely I'd always felt. Then my aunt asked me to help out at her salon, I guess to keep me busy, and I let myself be occupied. My tendency to gain weight forced me to exercise a lot, and between the salon, the kids, and Christmas dinners, one day I looked down at my hands and saw just how old they'd become. When I got divorced, I sold almost all the furniture in the house and prepared to move again, but my mother died a few months later. "Go and see what happened," she told me over and over in the ravings of her final days, and I knew exactly what it was she was asking me to do.

I packed a bag, took the ferry to Montevideo, and from there the bus to Atlántida. I rented a little house for a week, but almost five years have passed and I'm still here. What I learned at my aunt's salon in Buenos Aires, I now apply at this other salon where I work in Atlántida, right across from the Flamingo ice cream parlor. The photo of the last time we were there is still stuck with magnets to the water heater of my kitchen, our yellow overalls now almost beige from so many years. I don't go often to the beach, or get close to that rough sea. I prefer to always be at the salon, ready for when Pitys comes. I make sure she gets her bitter coffee, no cream, and I let everything happen in silence, doing my job with as little talk as possible. She sips her coffee while I rinse out the sand and poke carefully through her knots for more pebbles and shells. She doesn't meet my eyes, doesn't say thank you, doesn't pay. Each time, I show her in my open palm the three or four shells I've salvaged. She opens her hand and they drop from my palm into hers, like the little bones of minuscule creatures.

And then much more than a couple of weeks passes, maybe more than a month, until I conclude that Pitys has stopped coming. Something has happened, and every day I work with my full attention on the wait: Pitys has stopped coming. Until one night, after work, I gather my strength, pack up the shampoo and other things I'll need, and go to the house.

There is the pattern of green tiles under the roof, past the yard where we used to pet the Labrador to keep him from barking. During those years of washing her hair I'd sometimes imagined going into the house again, setting foot in the kitchen, the living room, the bedroom, that bathroom where we started our nightly sessions. Now I picture myself sitting Pitys down on her toilet again, wetting a towel to wash her face and armpits. I want to walk through those spaces again and see how much I can trust my memory, what condition things are in, if something of us still remains in the house. Something of my sister.

The door is open and I enter without knocking. The kitchen is the same kitchen, and the living room the same living room. Although the house is dark, I can tell how old and faded it all looks. There's a smaller sofa now, and some pictures have been taken down from the walls, leaving lighter ochre squares here and there. It's the same mess. Dirty dishes, empty bottles, books and clothes strewn everywhere, half-finished bags of potato chips. On the floor of the threshold between the living room and kitchen, there is a bag with four full bottles. I recognize the knot, that particular bow the man tied in the bags he used to bring her. I had seen him more than once around town, but I'd never considered the possibility that after all these years he still visited her.

I stand frozen for a moment in the hallway, wondering if it's really a good idea to keep going to the bedroom. I remember the cat, his yellow eyes staring at my sister, and in the silence I hear the fan. It's turning slowly, even after all these years. I cross the hallway and peer into the bedroom. It's dark and there is someone in the bed, under the sheets. The bed is the same, too large for that small room.

"Hello?" No doubt about it, that is Pitys's voice.

I glimpse her bare feet peeking out from the sheets, and I move closer and take hold of the metal bar my sister and I had once held on to.

"Oh!" she says. "Finally!"

She seems moved.

"Inspiration!"

Her feet stretch out for a moment. I grab hold of them, squeezing hard, maybe too hard for those delicate bones. But she doesn't protest. She is so cold I have to make an effort to stay where I am, and not let go of her again.

A VISIT FROM THE CHIEF

Lidia often went to the third floor of the Graziano Institute and sat down on the wooden bench there, right across from her mother's room. If she arrived after lunch had been distributed, most of the old people would be asleep, and then she could sit and read in silence for a long time with her back to the sun. Sometimes she dozed off, too. She almost never went in to see her mother, who in any case no longer recognized her. But Lidia thought it was important to spend some time at the home every week, just to keep an eye on things. If she stayed long enough a nurse would come by and Lidia could say hello, ask about any changes to her mother's medications, and let the nurse know when she'd be back next.

Lidia had gotten married and divorced, and, in between, she'd had a daughter who had used her very first paycheck to leave Buenos Aires and move to another continent. When Lidia realized her daughter wasn't coming back, she took out a mortgage on an apartment that never fully convinced her, but that promised to bind her to the vital responsibility of working until the last day of her life. Because at the time she had thought, *If this isn't how people cling to their lives, then how do they keep going?* She wished she knew someone in the same situation and could ask how they were coping, but she wasn't close enough to anyone to ask such a question.

In addition to her mother, Lidia had a job. Three hours in the morning, two in the afternoon. She went into the office on Tuesdays and worked from home the rest of the week. She had moved everything from her daughter's room into the new apartment and set it up just the way it had been in the old place, always ready for a possible visit that was ever more unlikely. In the meantime, she worked at her daughter's desk, the only one in the apartment. She would move the two pink quilted picture frames, the pencil holder, and the little ceramic box of lipsticks. If her daughter ever did come home, Lidia would be able to put it all back in the two minutes the elevator would take to reach the fourth floor. She liked to think that, every day, her daughter lent her that corner of the house, the only one where she seemed capable of concentrating.

At midmorning Lidia would settle in at her computer and answer customer emails as they came in. There were automatic replies for almost everything, all they needed was a small dose of personalization, and she had learned to think her own thoughts while she copied, edited, and sent. She wondered what it was all about—that is, what this whole business of living a life was even for. Was there something that one was supposed to understand at some point? Something that one was meant to see or do? She wasn't expecting any fantastic revelation. But if, after nearly sixty years of watching this dance which was still twirling before her eyes, there had been no sign that told her, "This is why you're here," "This is what must be understood," then was she really heading in the correct direction? Why did she do what she did? She went to the third floor of the Graziano Institute, sat on the last wooden bench, set her purse to her right and her coat to her left, and she read, because isn't that what people do when they've grown tired of waiting?

There she was, comfortable on her bench with her back to the sun and a book in her hand, when she saw an old woman coming down the hall toward her, headed for the elevators. The woman walked past, shuffling her skinny legs with determination. She wore the institute's gown tied at both sides and a pair of white sandals. Lidia saw the old woman stop after a few steps, then turn back toward her.

"Do you have any change?" she asked. "I need to take the train right away."

Lidia stood and checked her pockets. She knew she didn't have any change, she just wanted to show that she understood the old woman's problem and her intentions were good. The nurses were sure to come for the woman soon. Lidia smiled at her while she searched, and, in the performance, she was surprised to find three coins in her pocket. She pulled them out to see how much it was, but when she opened her hand, the old woman snatched the coins away.

"I'll pay you back," she said as she walked off down the hall.

Lidia watched the woman wait for the elevator, get on, and press a button. When the doors closed, the wall display showed the elevator's descent to the ground floor, where it stopped. She wondered how serious what had just happened might be, and considered notifying the nurses, though they were never easy to catch. She stood wavering in the middle of the hallway until she heard her mother moan and peeked timidly into the room to check on her.

"Mom," she said.

From the threshold, she watched her mother sleeping: the way she relaxed her jaw reminded Lidia of the way her daughter used to sleep. Maybe Lidia herself did the same thing, but it was impossible to know, because there was no one to see her asleep. The remains of her mother's lunch were piled on a tall tray table, which someone had rolled several feet away from the bed. Unlike the other patients' food, her mother's was now served on plastic dishes, ever since she had started smashing things on the floor. Lidia's mother was prone to fits of boiling rage. Serving the food on plastic and moving it away as soon as the meal was over helped save time on cleaning, and gave the rest of the patients a little peace and quiet. Maybe it was the memory of the last such scene Lidia had witnessed, but suddenly she felt terribly tired and decided it would be best to come back the next day. She returned to the hallway and gently closed her mother's door.

It was raining outside. Lidia covered her hair with a kerchief and tucked her bag under her arm to keep its contents dry. She wanted to get to her apartment and take off her shoes and pants. Though she hardly ever had any real appetite these days, she remembered she had some curry left over from the night before. She went down to the train station and saw the old woman on the platform, waiting distractedly on a bench. The hospital gown she still wore covered her body in front, but opened at the sides to reveal skinny white legs. Three young men were leering at her and laughing. Lidia went and sat down beside the woman, blocking the men's view. By then, the train was roaring into the station.

"I can take you back," Lidia offered, hoping the old woman would recognize her. Fearing that the woman couldn't hear well, she said it a second time, louder.

"Very kind of you," the old woman said as she stood up, "but I need to get home."

The train stopped, its doors opened, and the woman stepped onto a car. It was Lidia's train too, so she followed. She thought about calling the institute—she could wait with the woman at the next station until someone came to get her. If the old woman refused, though, Lidia wouldn't know what to do to make her stay.

On the train, other passengers stared at them. There was a woman who seemed about to offer help or ask what was wrong, and Lidia nodded at her as if to say, *It is what it is, we must be patient,* and the woman seemed to understand and didn't look their way again. Lidia almost wished she'd tried a little harder.

Lidia was struck that no one moved to give their seat to the old woman. Perhaps it was because she held so tightly to the handrail, seeming to obstinately ignore her own fragility, or maybe it was just that her attention was on what was happening outside. At each stop, the train braked and the old woman's head tilted from side to side as she looked for station names and peered at the map of the subway line. She seemed to be struggling to figure out where she was.

Twice, Lidia asked the old woman if this was her stop, and both times the woman said no, it was the next one. When she got to her own stop, Lidia was unnerved to see the old woman also preparing to get off the train.

Lidia tried to walk beside the woman and start some kind of conversation, but the old woman was desperately slow, and when they were halfway up the stairs Lidia simply sped up and went out to the street, leaving her behind. Although the rain had lessened a little, she paused under a shop awning. She felt responsible, and that inability to free herself from other people's problems filled her with exasperation. The old woman was taking the last step so laboriously that Lidia had no choice but to go back to her and ask what she planned to do next.

"I'm going home," the old woman said, "I already told you!"

"But where *is* your house?"

The woman sucked in air as though summoning all her patience and drew herself up straighter, then glanced to either side while exhaling all the air she'd taken in, until her body returned to its initial curve. It was such a cartoonish gesture that Lidia felt her own brusqueness, sensed the tedium she was inflicting on the old woman with her questions, instead of doing something useful to help her.

"Do you like white tea?" Lidia asked. "If you want some, I live just around the corner."

—

Once in the apartment, Lidia helped the old woman remove her sandals, gave her a towel so that she could dry her shoulders and chest, and lent her a light cardigan to wear over the hospital gown. She would make the tea and then call the institute. No one could accuse her of anything other than trying to help, and if the old woman told them where the train money had come from, Lidia would just deny it. She sat the woman down at the dining table in the living room and went to the kitchen. While she waited for the water to boil, new questions occurred to her. Did the woman have children? How long had she been in the institute? Did she by chance know Lidia's mother? But when she carried in the tray with tea and some cookies, she found the old woman watching the blank TV screen. Lidia switched it on, and they drank the tea in silence. For months now, it had been impossible for Lidia to do that kind of thing with her own mother.

They watched a news story about the noisiest cities in Latin America, then an interview with two Ukrainian soldiers. When the reporter asked the soldiers how long they thought the war would last, the old woman said, "See how handsome Joel looks?" And for the first time, she smiled.

After two minutes of the weather forecast, Lidia went to the kitchen to call the institute.

"Graziano," a voice answered.

"I think I found a patient of yours," Lidia said.

"Do you mean a person who should be here?" There was no surprise in the voice on the phone. "One moment, please."

She was transferred twice before she spoke with a doctor

who described a "presumed runaway" and asked if it was the patient who was with her. Lidia peered into the living room to get another look at the old woman. The description was neither accurate nor fair, but she knew it was this old woman, so she said yes.

Back in the living room, she sat down at the table beside the woman and explained that she had called the institute. She tried to get a sense of whether the old woman understood what she was saying, but her face held no clues.

"The problem," Lidia told her, "is that they can't come to get you."

The institute's insurance required that patients be moved only by ambulance, and at the moment none were available.

"They said to call tomorrow morning to coordinate the pickup," Lidia explained. She realized how annoyed she herself was with this news, but she tried not to let it show. "Do you understand? You'll have to spend the night here. I hope that won't be a problem . . ."

"What about Joel?"

Lidia shook her head, wondering what she would feed the woman.

"He's always late, but he always comes," the old woman said.

What if the woman followed a strict diet and she gave her something that was off-limits? Lidia realized she didn't know what her mother's diet was, or if she even followed one. And where would the old woman sleep? On the sofa? In her daughter's room? Would she actually sleep? Or would she spend the whole night wandering around? Should Lidia help her bathe or get undressed? She thought maybe she should lock up the apartment and keep the keys with her in her room. She regretted bringing the woman home with her. The leftover curry wouldn't be enough for both of them. Lidia went to the refrigerator to see what she could cook, and then the doorbell startled her.

"It's Joel," the old woman called.

Lidia went to the intercom and lifted the receiver.

"Yes?"

She could hear the sound of people on the street.

"I'm sorry to disturb you," a male voice said. "But is it possible my mother is there with you?"

Lidia glanced down the hall in alarm. How could this be? Had someone followed them? Had the institute called him and given him her address?

"It's my sandal." The old woman's voice reached her from the dining table, though Lidia couldn't see her. "The left one."

Lidia looked at the sandals she had taken off the old woman and placed by the door. Without putting down the receiver, she picked up the left one. It had a plastic button the size of a watch battery, and on the inside of the strap, there was a message: "If you find my mother, please press the locator :-)."

The doorbell rang again and she buzzed the building's front door open. She wondered if she would have enough food for three people, and immediately chastised herself for such a stupid question. She smoothed her hair in front of the mirror where she hung her keys. She was tired, and angry, and nervous, all at the same time, and it was too late to go to the grocery store. In the worst-case scenario she'd have to order delivery. And just how old would this man be? She peered out into the hallway, where she could hear him climbing the stairs.

"He doesn't take elevators," the old woman said.

Lidia had an urge to close the door. She could still lock it and not open it again—that was entirely within her rights. But the old woman had come over to the door. With cold hands, she weakly pushed Lidia aside, and now she was out in the hallway.

"Joel!"

Lidia saw the man walk up and let himself be hugged. He was slender and tall, more than a head taller than the old woman. His skin had a slightly orangish hue, like that of people she sometimes saw coming out of tanning salons. The old woman waved the man inside, but he politely turned to Lidia first, humbly waiting for her permission.

"Of course, come in," she found herself obliged to say. "Please."

And now the man was inside.

He must have been about fifteen years younger than Lidia. Not young, but there was a distinct spring in his movements. He looked curiously down the hallway toward the bedrooms, and then back at his mother with a smile.

"What happened, Mom? How is it possible that people still give you money?"

"You just have to know how to ask for it," the old woman said.

Lidia gave silent thanks that she said no more than that. She asked the man if he wanted some tea, and he accepted. While she was making it, she could hear them talking and laughing in the other room. She was using more white tea today than in the whole previous month. Did she really have to feed him dinner, too? Was it still her responsibility to take care of the old woman, or could she simply leave her in this man's custody? She thought about calling the institute again, but realized that the man would hear her talking.

While they drank the tea he asked Lidia some questions. Where she'd found his mother, if she lived alone in that apartment, if she had any kids. But as soon as Lidia started to answer, he seemed to lose interest. He was much more enthusiastic about talking than listening. He discussed his own life by asking himself questions and then immediately answering them.

He told her that he owned a gym behind the mall, and then asked himself, but was the gym really his, or was he just an employee? It was 100 percent his. And it wasn't the muscles or the weights that he liked, it was confronting his own limitations every day, and overcoming them. Was that something he could teach other people? Of course it was, that's why he owned a gym.

"We saw you on TV," the old woman told him. "You were very good."

He nodded absently and kept talking. Sometimes the people who came to the gym couldn't even stand up straight. People who were young but had already given up. People who were divorced, tired, in debt, ill fed, disappointed with their own choices. Had he made good choices? He didn't know—who was he to say?—but he did know that he could help others, and it was knowledge that demanded a commitment.

"You looked very handsome," the old woman said.

He moved more than necessary as he talked. He seemed aware of every part of his body, of the T-shirt tight over his chest and arms but loose in the abdominal area, of his straight spine, his white teeth, his hair, which was meticulously messy on top but carefully buzzed at the edges of his forehead and the nape of his neck.

The old woman asked to go to the bathroom but declined Lidia's offer of assistance, so Lidia just pointed her to the second door down the hall. Lidia watched the old woman make an effort to stand up, distracted now from her son's monologue, and heard her walk slowly away, dragging her feet until she found the bathroom and closed the door. Then Lidia interrupted the man and told him that she had called the institute.

"Did you give them your address? Or your phone number? Did they ask for it?"

"Not exactly."

The man seemed to intuit that they hadn't offered to come pick his mother up, either. She told him they'd asked her to take care of the woman and said they would pick her up the next morning.

"She runs away all the time," he said. "I think they figure she'll just get lost for good one of these days."

Lidia thought about telling him that she understood, and that her mother was also a patient at the institute, but she was afraid he would suspect she'd had something to do with the old woman's escape and she held her tongue.

"I'm going to check on my mother," he said.

She liked that he said "my mother" instead of "Mom." It felt more respectful, and she knew how hard it was to maintain that respect for senile people. She put the empty mugs on the tray and carried everything into the kitchen. When she came back, the living room was still empty. She glanced down the hall and saw the closed bathroom door. The light in the last bedroom, her daughter's room, was on.

The man was lying on the bed with his arms behind his head and his eyes closed. He hadn't taken off his sneakers. His feet were crossed on top of the flowered bedspread, and he was moving them rhythmically, humming something to himself. Lidia cleared her throat, and he opened just one eye first, as though spying on her, and then smiled and sat up, swinging his legs down from the bed.

"I'm so sorry," he said, though he didn't seem embarrassed. "My mother is still in the bathroom."

There was the sound of a flush and the bathroom door opened. Lidia wanted the man to get off her daughter's bed, but since he didn't move, she decided to remain standing in the doorway. The old woman approached and walked right past her into the room.

"Joel?"

"I'm here, Mom," he said. He didn't get up but reached out his arms to her, offering a hug.

The old woman went over to him, took hold of his head, and kissed his forehead. She sat down beside him and rested her temple on his shoulder. Lidia didn't want them in her daughter's bedroom, but there was something touching about that love, which seemed so real.

"Again, I'm sorry," he said, "really. Do you know why I apologize twice?"

"Because you never seem like you mean it," the old woman said.

He held her against his body, cradling her.

"I hope everything is okay with your daughter," he said.

"Oh, yes, she's just traveling. She could come back any time."

The man ran a finger over the wooden headboard.

"Long trip," he said, looking at the dust on his finger.

Lidia was still on the threshold of the room; she needed to sit down, but was resolved to remain on her feet.

"Want me to tell you what I think?" he asked, wiping his finger on his pants.

What she wanted was to know when they were going to leave her house.

"I know people, see? It's what I do."

He stared at her until she averted her eyes.

"I think you're scared. You want to know how you're scared?" He raised a hand, the palm open toward the floor. "You are this leaf. The wind blows it this way and that." His hand moved fluidly from side to side, suspended above her daughter's daisy rug. "See how that little leaf lets itself be carried along? You know why the leaf lets the wind do what it wants?"

"Maybe the wind is life?" Lidia hadn't meant to be sarcastic, and she was uncomfortable with how sarcastic she'd just sounded.

His hand hung motionless in the air. It wore two thick rings and had a small cross tattooed on the index finger's second knuckle.

"I'm asking you, will the little leaf dare to hear the truth?"

She thought about what she would do if the man became violent. Should she call the police? The idea made her feel exposed. She remembered she had a magnet with emergency phone numbers stuck to the refrigerator; she could recall the color and the font, but she was nervous now and could not think of the numbers themselves.

"I'm going to tell you," said the man. "I'm going to tell you the truth."

The old woman had fallen asleep, and he laid her gently down on the mattress. She grunted and settled in, and he got up, lifted her legs onto the bed, and covered them with the other end of the bedspread.

"It lets itself be carried along because it's afraid of being broken. Of not being flexible enough, understand?"

The man took a step toward Lidia, and she let go of the doorway and stepped backward. Again, he put his hand out between the two of them.

"Young leaves can bend like this." He closed and opened his fingers over his palm, showing her just how attentive one could be to such a movement. "Dry leaves . . . well, they are more prone to breaking, I'll give you that."

She thought about the locator chip attached to the sandal strap, about the doctor's description of the old woman, about how her own mother, before throwing dishes to the floor, would suddenly open her eyes and mouth wide, as though the crash had reached her a few seconds early, or she were desperately anticipating it.

"But you are much stronger than you think." He looked her up and down, studying her body part by part, and nodded, as if confirming his assessment. "And I'm here to prove that to you."

The man took another step toward her, and she made a huge effort not to shrink away. He came very close to her without leaving the bedroom, and he smelled like the plastic of new things. She could feel her heart pounding fast, but events in the bedroom were unfolding so slowly that she was able to pay real attention to them all, to contemplate and meditate on the details. What was happening was strange, but she was more surprised by the calm with which she was confronting it.

"You're going to go to the front door and you'll open the bag I left on the floor there. And what is the little leaf going to find in the nice man's bag? A present. Get it and bring it to me."

He didn't wait for her to reply, but turned his back to Lidia and started examining her daughter's bookshelves, his tattooed index finger caressing the spines of the books that caught his eye. Lidia walked away. If she stopped for a second in the kitchen, she could look at the magnet on the fridge; she'd have to try hard to remember the number for the police until she got a chance to dial it. She saw the bag on the floor, picked it up, and carried it to the kitchen, where she memorized the number. Now, where was her phone?

"So? Did you find the present?" the man asked from the bedroom, barely raising his voice.

She set the bag on the counter and unzipped it. She realized what she had to do. She would simply leave the apartment. If the elevator took too long, he would catch her immediately on the stairs, and if that happened she would scream. Would the neighbors come out? How long would it take them? Lidia opened the bag. She saw the tip of a metal barrel and knew it was a gun before she took it out.

"Radio silence," said the man's voice. "The wind carries the leaf this way and that . . . Bring in your spoils, let's see!"

She had to move carefully as she took the gun from the bag, because she was shaking and didn't want any accidents. She'd seen enough movies to know that this was the moment when she needed to brandish the gun and threaten the man—all she had to do was immobilize him with a bullet to the leg and then run out of the apartment and start banging on doors in the hallway. But she knew she wouldn't do it.

She returned to the bedroom with the weight of the gun in her two hands. The old woman was still sleeping, and Lidia wondered if she might be dead. The woman had turned or been turned toward the wall, and her chest was as still as the rest of the room. But where had the man gone? The sound of the toilet flush told her the bathroom door was now open. The man came into the bedroom buttoning his pants, and glanced quickly at his mother.

"Come on into the living room," he said, and snatched the gun away without an ounce of caution as he passed her.

He walked off; Lidia followed.

"Have a seat, please. Make yourself at home," he said.

He pointed her toward the armchair and sat down on the sofa at the end closest to her. The TV was muted and still tuned to the news.

"I know you don't like me and I know you think I'm a liar. But I really do own a gym, I do love my mother, my mother does get lost again and again, and I do help people improve. Because I like to do it, period." He waved the gun carelessly as he spoke. "It's like a hobby, you know?"

He was staring at her, so she nodded.

"And sometimes, when I need money, I look for a way to fill my wallet, like everyone else. Isn't that stealing? No, stealing means taking money from people without giving anything in return, and I, as you must have realized, have a lot to give. What do we have to learn here? Well, that the two things are not mutually exclusive. Do you have money in the house?"

She nodded.

"Can you give me an idea of how much, more or less?"

"I have six hundred dollars in the dresser in my room."

He stared at her, waiting.

"And some jewelry, in the same drawer."

"You'll also give me your card."

She nodded and started to get up, but he stopped her by gently resting his hand on her knee.

"Wait, not yet."

On TV, the interview with the two Ukrainian soldiers was replaying. The man's hand was still on her knee. He gave it a few pats, and she wondered if he was planning to rape her. When she was young, she'd occasionally thought that such a thing could happen to her, but it had been years since the idea had crossed her mind.

"Sorry," he said, and took his hand away.

"Did you do something to that lady? Should we call an ambulance?"

"To my mother?" He laughed.

The man stared at the Ukrainian soldiers for a moment, attentive to the mouths of those mute men talking over each other. She breathed, his distraction a sudden respite, but she took in so much air she had to sit up straighter. Her spine stretched, her lungs inflated, and, even so, the air kept coming in. When she exhaled, she also let out a sincere sigh, and with the sigh her eyes filled with tears. She wiped them away with the back of her hand.

"Don't worry so much," said the man, his eyes still on the TV. "We'll only stay the one night. I don't like to wake my mother up once she falls asleep. You should get some rest too. You'll see, tomorrow you'll have the most normal kind of day."

He turned toward her and patted the sofa cushion beside him. Lidia didn't move. He kissed the gun and winked at her, then patted the sofa again, so she got up from the armchair and sat beside him, though as far away as she could.

"Perfect," he said with a nod. "I see you're starting to understand how I like things."

He stretched out the length of the sofa with his feet up and his head in her lap. She jerked her hands away, taking care not to touch him. It was a heavy, hot head, and seeing that face upside down, from above, was like looking at the underbelly of a giant worm. His eyes were below his mouth, and they were gazing up at her. His eyelashes were too long. His mouth seemed far away, damp and small, as though misplaced.

"Can you scratch my head?" he asked. "It helps me sleep." He crossed his hands over his stomach, the gun between them, and closed his eyes. "Scratch, please." He tapped his fingertips on the gun barrel. "Scratch."

Lidia brought a hand to his curly hair and carefully sank her fingers in, moving them slowly over his skull. She tried to do it without thinking, like when she cut open a whole chicken and had to break the two joints between the foot and thigh; just as with the chicken, she tried to breathe as little as possible with this man. The less she smelled, the less she felt what she was doing. She knew that even upside down, she would remember that face for the rest of her life. She would have been able to describe it to the police without hesitation, in full detail, except that he knew where she lived. She thought about her daughter, about what would happen if her daughter were to call right now. Lidia would have no way to communicate that she was in danger. It had never occurred to her that they might need to agree on a code, a safe word like "salty" or "darling," to let the other know that something wasn't right. How could they have lived together all those years without a code word?

"Before I take your money and give you back your phone, I want to do something for you. Is there anything you need?" He nodded, waiting without opening his eyes.

Lidia thought about her mother. By that time she would have eaten dinner, and a nurse would have tucked her in and turned the TV to the documentary channel, which was the one that put her mother to sleep the fastest.

"We have all the time in the world. Tell me how I can help you."

If the man killed her that night, Lidia thought in alarm, the news might take days to reach the institute.

"Speak," he said.

And if the news did finally reach her mother, would she understand? Would it be enough to tell her once, or would she forget right away? Would it hurt her again each time it was explained?

"Speak, I'm telling you."

She had to say something; the man had opened his eyes and his voice had hardened. And her daughter—how long would it take for the news to reach her? How would they find her? Would she visit her grandmother? Would her grandmother recognize her?

The man jolted upright and looked at Lidia, furious now for the first time. She wanted to speak—she had to speak. He stood up, pointed the gun at her head, and removed the safety. It was such a stunning moment that she had trouble reacting.

"You old bitch, tell me how I can fucking help you."

She wanted to open her mouth, anything would do, but she didn't know what to say. The man kicked the coffee table, and it fell over and broke in two, sending magazines flying. She closed her eyes. In the darkness, she heard him approach, and she dreaded the new-plastic smell. She inhaled and there it was, stronger than ever. She felt the cold barrel slowly come to rest against her temple. She thought about where the bullet would exit if it went in, and she realized she couldn't answer, that she wasn't thinking straight.

"Nothing?" he shouted. "There's nothing I can help you with? You think I'm some kind of dumbass?"

He kicked something else, but she was too terrified to open her eyes and see what it was. She heard a slight click and then a bang. Had he fired? She tried to detect whether she felt any pain, whether the bang could have been a bullet that had gone into her head. Was she dead? Was this how she was going to die? She wanted to open her eyes, but the terror kept them closed. But there *had* been a bang. A noise, and then nothing. She opened her eyes.

"Do you think I'm a piece of shit? You think I can't do anything for an old bag like you? What the fuck have I been saying ever since I walked into this shitty apartment, huh? What the fuck do I do for a living?"

"The lamp," Lidia said. Her eyes turned to the lamp that hung over the table to show him what she was talking about. "Can you fix it?"

He turned around, slowly dropping the hand holding the gun, and went over to the table. He seemed to be studying the lamp, but suddenly he leaned toward the sideboard, stretching oddly over the porcelain knickknacks there, and with one swipe knocked them all to the floor. He kicked a chair over, stomped on it, broke its wooden backrest, yanked out a piece of wood, and, brandishing the jagged end, he came menacingly toward her.

"What kind of fucking asshole do you think I am?"

It was the strangest thing—she didn't seem to be scared anymore. There had been a bang, right? So was she even alive?

"You know what the problem with people is?" He had the wooden stake in one hand and the gun in the other and was threatening her with both. "They all go around asking for things. You'd think the gym was the fucking customer-service line straight to the Chief himself. 'I want tighter glutes,' 'I need to lose weight,' 'I have to walk ten thousand steps a day.' I want, I need, I have to. But what about me? I'm the fucking specialist! You think I didn't train for this? You think I didn't train for this? You think I don't try every goddamned fucking thing I recommend? Open that fucking mouth, dammit! Do you or do you not believe that?"

"Joel?"

The old woman had gotten up and was clutching the hallway door frame.

"When he gets mad, he curses," she said, "but he's not really like that."

Lidia took the chance to stand up. He started shouting again as soon as he saw her on her feet. "A fucking lamp? That's what you need?"

"Joel," the old woman said.

"Tell me your shitty problem! Open your fucking mouth!"

"My daughter scares me," Lidia said. Her voice shook like crepe paper. "When she was a baby . . ."

"What? What is it?"

He took a quick step toward her and pushed her back down.

"Tell me, goddammit!"

"I don't know!" Sitting on the sofa again made her feel desperate. Would she never be able to stand up?

The man tossed the wooden stake aside and leaned over her; he was huge. He took her by the shoulders and shook her violently.

"Open that fucking mouth!" He pushed her back against the sofa cushions and grabbed her jaw.

"I hated her."

"I can't understand you." He was so close he seemed about to kiss her.

"I hated her so much as a baby." Lidia had trouble talking with his fingers pressing her cheeks into her teeth so she couldn't close her mouth.

She tried to speak anyway. He squeezed harder.

"I had to learn to love her," she said. "Now I love her so much—too much, even. It was a trap."

He brought his lips to her ear and whispered, "It's not my little fingers that are hurting you."

He squeezed harder and she tasted blood between her teeth.

"What hurts?" he yelled.

She had the urge to scream, but it was impossible.

"Her resentment," Lidia said, and he released her.

She felt her mouth numb with pain, and, at the same time, loosened: "My daughter's resentment is like . . ."

He raised a hand to silence her.

"It's done," he said.

She closed her mouth and he walked a few steps away. Neither of them spoke.

Then he set the gun down on the table. He pressed the fingertips of one hand against those of the other and then pulled them apart, as though stretching out invisible gum. Maybe he was going to say something, but finally he just gestured, opening his hands with the palms down, apparently an appeal for calm. Then he lay on the floor, bent his knees, and started doing sit-ups. He did sets of five different exercises and then lay belly-up for a while, his arms and legs splayed, as his agitated body gradually relaxed. Every once in a while he looked at the lamp, still hanging from the ceiling. He was panting, and his eyes closed and then opened again.

Once he had composed himself, he got up and stretched his neck to either side. He went over to his mother, who was admiring him distractedly, and smoothed a curl of tangled hair on the right side of her head. He took her by the shoulders and seemed to want to sit her down somewhere, but, in the disaster he had sown, only the sofa was free. He patiently led the old woman over to sit on the end opposite Lidia. He looked around for the light switch, turned it off, and walked back toward them. He started to sit between them, but then lay down instead, this time with his head on his mother's lap and his feet on Lidia's. The old woman sank her fingers into his hair to scratch his head and settled in with a sigh. She closed her eyes and leaned her head against the wall, scratching all the while.

Lidia sat for a long time staring at the now darkened apartment, feeling the weight of the man's legs on hers. If she got up, she would wake him. The gun was on the table, and the stake—where was the stake? She forced herself to take a few breaths, counting to seven on the inhale and nine on the exhale, trying to relax her body. She dropped her shoulders, concentrated on the feeling of the soles of her feet against the floor. She didn't need to relax—she needed to confirm that she was still alive. She knew that the exercise was working once she realized where the bullet could have exited. She had the urge to touch her head, to corroborate, but she didn't dare. Instead she leaned it against the wall like the old woman, rested her arms to either side of her body, avoiding the man's legs, and closed her eyes. For a good while, it was so quiet in the apartment that she could hear the traffic on the avenue below.

"Know what I did before I had the gym?"

She opened her eyes. His were still closed. The desperation rushed back in.

"Close your eyes," he ordered.

She did.

"I'm asking you a question."

"Sorry, I'm distracted. I think . . ."

"I asked if you knew what I did before I had the gym."

She made an effort to think, because maybe she did know, maybe he had mentioned it at some point.

"Do you or don't you know? Is it that hard?"

"What did you do?"

"I hung on the sides of buildings to clean windows."

Lidia heard him sigh deeply, as though nostalgic. He cleared his throat and she thought, *Here comes the window washer story.*

But he said, "You know, one night, when I was seven years old, my father told me about how when he was my age, he'd taken a cat that lived in his tenement, carried it up to the fifth floor, held it out a window, and dropped it. He told me the cat survived, but it could only walk with its front legs. You know why I'm telling you this?"

It took her a few seconds to realize that she was supposed to answer.

"Don't open your eyes," he said.

"Why are you telling me this?"

"Because of what my father said next, something he explained to me. You want to know what he said?"

"What did he say?"

"That from then on the cat would lie in the doorways of apartments, but wouldn't go inside. And that if it lay in a doorway it meant that someone from that place was going to die. Then, sooner or later, in two days or in a year, someone died, and everyone would be watching to see which doorway the cat went to sleep in next."

"The cat knew who was going to die?" she asked.

"How could it know? No. It was my dad who moved the cat. He said it was easy to know whose turn it was. It wasn't a sixth sense or anything—it just took paying real attention."

"What if someone died suddenly, in an accident?"

"That did happen, but people figured that the cat indicated

death sentences that were ordained from on high, and accidents were something else, not the work of the Chief himself. But I asked my dad that same question. And I asked if he believed in ghosts, in dead people who come back, in living people who go around dead—well, all that stuff. And you know what he said?"

"What did he say?"

"That he did. My father! He said of course he believed, and that was why we had to deal with them. Can you imagine? And you know what the funniest thing is? You know what it is? I'm asking you."

"Sorry, right. What's the funniest thing?"

"That he disappeared. Like a ghost, get it? So there I was one day, twenty years later, hanging from a platform and cleaning windows at the Imperial Hotel, and suddenly I see something amazing. Do you know the Imperial? Thick windows, two layers at least, because of the street noise. I stopped cleaning and looked inside, using my hands like visors. It was a deluxe room, queen bed, desk, reading chair, lamps everywhere. And who was in there unbuttoning his shirt? It was me, myself, and I."

"What do you mean, it was you?"

"It was me, thirty years older. But I'm telling you, I was so stunned at first, I didn't realize it was my dad. It was a shock, like seeing someone you've known your whole life and at the same time you're acutely aware that you don't know him at all. It was like coming face-to-face with the Chief himself. So, he unbuttons the last button and looks at me. But he looks at me without any surprise, and walks toward me, and I'm wondering if he can really see me through the glass. Now he's so close that if the window was open I could touch him. I could grab hold of him if the ropes suddenly came loose from the beam; he was so close he could have saved me. But he drew the curtains. He closed them."

For a few seconds the man said nothing more. Lidia opened her eyes. The lights from the building across the way had gone out, and everything was darker now.

"Understand?"

"Yes," she said.

"What do you understand?"

She was really thinking about it. There was something she couldn't quite grasp yet, like earlier with the place where the bullet would have exited. But just as with that place, maybe all she needed was a little more time.

"Give me a minute, please."

"Of course," he said.

And the two of them sat there in silence. Lidia went back over the story, but soon she was thinking again about her mother and daughter, and then she felt so tired that she couldn't resolve anything in particular about them, either. She realized that if he wasn't going to leave, then she needed to disappear. And maybe it was the silence, the fact that he had finally stopped talking, that made her muscles give in to the exhaustion. She wondered whether she was actually capable of falling asleep in a situation like that, and a second later, she had done it.

—

When Lidia woke up, the man wasn't there. The daylight hurt her eyes for a moment, and her body felt stiff. She had to move slowly. At the other end of the sofa, the old woman was sleeping with her head lolling to one side.

There were noises coming from the kitchen, and the smell of coffee. The ceramic and porcelain shards on the floor had been swept against the wall. The broken chair had been picked up and placed in the hallway. She looked around for the gun but didn't see it. The light wasn't only coming in through the window: the defective lamp was now illuminated. It was the first time in years that she'd seen it turned on. Its plastic shade had a soft and satiny translucence, and its light shone onto a dish towel spread on the table, along with jam jars, the butter dish, the milk, and the little mug without a handle that she used as a sugar bowl. The man came in with three plates that he set on the table.

"Eggs," he said.

He looked rested and refreshed, and it seemed he'd wet the sides of his hair to style it. The old woman shifted at her end of the sofa, opened her eyes, and glanced around, disoriented.

"Do you have any money?" she asked Lidia. "I need to take the train right away."

It was unclear whether she was asking for real, or joking.

"Eggs, Mom."

He went over and helped his mother up. The old woman seemed annoyed as she chastised him: "You think I don't know how to find my own way home? Huh?"

They walked together to the table, where he slid out a chair for her and pushed one of the plates toward her.

"All set," he said, handing his mother some silverware.

The old woman took a bite. He was still standing beside her, and he poured her some coffee. Only then did he turn toward Lidia.

"Please," he said. "Come on, there's enough for everyone."

Lidia stood up. Despite her numbness, there was something unexpectedly buoyant in her movements. In the lamplight, the apartment didn't seem entirely familiar; it felt warmer and cozier than usual. The man sat down across from his mother and started to eat. He had set Lidia's plate at the head of the table; she knew she couldn't eat a bite, but she went over and sat down anyway. She rubbed her face with the palms of her hands. The man poured her some coffee, and she drank it while she watched mother and son finish their breakfast.

"I took the money from the dresser, and the jewelry and card. I left your phone on your daughter's nightstand. Is there anything else I can do for you?"

Lidia slowly shook her head.

After slinging his bag over his shoulder and helping his mother with her sandals, he turned to her.

"It's a shame it has to be this way," he said. "But even if you need me, don't try to find me. The best thing for someone like you is to never hear from me again."

She nodded. He nodded, too, in farewell. He offered his arm to his mother, who took it, and without another word they walked to the front door. Lidia waited until she heard it click shut, and then she sat picturing it for a long time—white, closed, and motionless—as though trying to remember it. When she was convinced they really were gone, she slowly leaned over to confirm it.

She thought she could burst out crying, or run to her daughter's room, climb into bed, and sleep for the rest of the day. But she couldn't manage to stand up. She looked around, searching the floor and the walls for a hole, a mark. Because there had been a bang, that possibility still existed, even though none of the neighbors had had the decency to come check on her. And if she didn't find the hole, did that mean she was dead?

Then she noticed the eggs, still there in front of her. She picked up a fork and took a bite, and then another, and another. She had finished the plate before she grasped just how hungry she was. So hungry she wondered if there was anything else in the fridge that she could eat, and she was surprised to realize that, without even thinking about it, she was on her feet again.

Notes on the Stories

I wrote "Welcome to the Club" thinking about my friend Martina, who passed away years ago and was so present as I wrote this story.

I saw the horse in "A Fabulous Animal" in Hurlingham, the neighborhood where I grew up. I saw dozens of them, and I dedicate the story to all of them.

"William in the Window" did happen. It is perhaps the most autobiographical story I've written, and perhaps also, for that reason, it's better not to say any more.

Though there is nothing autobiographical in "An Eye in the Throat," I want to dedicate that story to my nephew Logan, who suffered a similar accident at the same age.

I wrote "The Woman from Atlántida" thinking about my sister Pamela and my cousins Deborah and Estafanía, childhood playmates with whom I so often snuck into other people's yards, and shouted "Incoming!" in the Atlántida sea.

I met the man from "A Visit from the Chief" during a long stay in Barcelona. Although we never saw eye to eye, with him I finally learned how to lift weights without hurting my lower back. It seems like a small thing, but I'll be forever grateful.

Acknowledgments

Thanks to Vera Giaconi, for the privilege of your friendship and your reading.

And to Nora Riccardi, for sharing your experience working with children with speech-language disorders; and to Miguel Chimski, who explained seven times, with infinite patience, how to correctly skin a hare. Without them, the stories "An Eye in the Throat" and "Welcome to the Club" wouldn't have been the same.

Thanks to my editors Ana Laura Pérez and Elena Ramírez, for their close and generous readings, for their patience and kindness.

Thanks to Anne Meadows, Mary Mount and Orla King from Picador, for believing in my work.

Thanks to my English translator Megan McDowell, for caring so much, so seriously, so kindly.

Thanks to my literary agent Johanna Castillo, for that divine strength of hers, and for all her confidence.

Acknowledgments

Thanks to my dear ones: Svein, Anita, Sebastián, Isabel, and Julieta, patient readers and life companions. I write above all for you, so you will love me as much as I can get you to love me.

And to my family: We seem to live so far apart, but as time passes I feel we are ever closer.

About the Translator

Megan McDowell has translated many of the most important Spanish-language writers working today. Her translations have won the National Book Award for Translated Literature and the English PEN Award, and have been nominated for the International Booker Prize (four times). In 2020, she won an Award in Literature from the American Academy of Arts and Letters.

'Remarkably taut, clear, precise, and yet capable of capturing the extent of our human messiness, these stories are perfect for the times we dwell inside'
Colum McCann, author of *Apeirogon*

'No one writes like Samanta Schweblin. Her narratives are sui generis – wonderfully unpredictable and invitingly strange'
Lorrie Moore, author of *I Am Homeless if This Is Not My Home*

'These stories understand the secret moments and strange connections that resonate through a person's life – and they explore these intimacies with a razor-sharp edge. Samanta Schweblin is at the top of her game'
Heather Parry, author of *Carrion Crow*

'These beautifully crafted and eerily unsettling stories completely hypnotized me. This is the sort of storytelling which resonates in the head, the heart and all mysterious parts in between. I wish I could write like this'
Jan Carson, author of *The Raptures*

'Samanta Schweblin has a rare ability to write stories that are more than just stories . . . She understands the delicate and monstrous music that is shaped from our shadows, from the ghosts we carry within us. That is why to read her is to remember; to read her is to witness, in bewilderment, a miracle made of disturbance and light'
Agustina Bazterrica, author of *Tender Is the Flesh*

'From the very first lines of the first story, these stories grip with a real and disturbing power. Dark currents pulse through Samanta Schweblin's cool and poised prose in this immaculate translation by Megan McDowell. The effect of reading the whole collection is akin to being trapped in a hall of mirrors – seeing reflections and distortions, half-glimpsing things, hearing screams'
Lucy Caldwell, author of *These Days*

'The atmosphere in these stories, crafted with striking clarity, foreshadows that, at some point, everything will go awry and the effects of that twist will haunt the protagonists forever. These are not ghost stories. They are something far worse and far better: they are stories about human beings'
Leila Guerriero, author of *La Llamada*

'A book of finely wrought tales exploring family, grief, love, and longing'
i newspaper

'Bravura . . . standout . . . eerie and remarkably moving . . . [you will find yourself] in the space on the other side of terror – a space of openness, fragility and strange reassurance'
The Guardian

'[Schweblin's stories] seem to hover, indeed like fever dreams, between the reassuring familiarities of domestic life and the stark, unpredictable, visionary flights of the unconscious. Everything exists in a state of tension, charged with contradictions'
Joyce Carol Oates, *The New York Times Book Review*

'Schweblin, a master of the uncanny, keeps us in this kind of ever-shifting gray area between the two poles of her title'
The New Yorker

'The tissue between ordinary life and the catastrophic is gossamer-fine, and we know the rupture must come . . . If there is a lesson, it is perhaps that usually we survive'
Francesca Segal, *Financial Times*

GOOD AND EVIL AND OTHER STORIES

Samanta Schweblin won the 2022 National Book Award for Translated Literature for her story collection *Seven Empty Houses*. Her debut novel, *Fever Dream*, was shortlisted for the International Booker Prize, and her novel *Little Eyes*, and story collection *Mouthful of Birds*, have been longlisted for the same prize. Her books have been translated into more than forty languages, and her stories have appeared in English in *The New Yorker*, *The Paris Review*, *Granta*, *Harper's Magazine* and elsewhere. Originally from Buenos Aires, Schweblin lives in Berlin. *Good and Evil and Other Stories* is her third collection.

Also by Samanta Schweblin

Fever Dream

Mouthful of Birds

Little Eyes

Seven Empty Houses